My School on the Hill

Ruskin Bond is known for his signature simplistic and witty writing style. He is the author of several bestselling short stories, novellas, collections, essays and children's books; and has contributed a number of poems and articles to various magazines and anthologies. At the age of twenty-three, he won the prestigious John Llewellyn Rhys Prize for his first novel, *The Room on the Roof*. He was also the recipient of the Padma Shri in 1999, Lifetime Achievement Award by the Delhi Government in 2012 and the Padma Bhushan in 2014.

Born in 1934, Ruskin Bond grew up in Jamnagar, Shimla, New Delhi and Dehradun. Apart from three years in the UK, he has spent all his life in India, and now lives in Landour, Mussoorie, with his adopted family.

RUSKIN BOND

My School on the Hill

RUPA

Published by
Rupa Publications India Pvt. Ltd 2022
7/16, Ansari Road, Daryaganj
New Delhi 110002

Sales centres:
Allahabad Bengaluru Chennai
Hyderabad Jaipur Kathmandu
Kolkata Mumbai

ISBN: 978-93-5520-174-4

First impression 2022

10 9 8 7 6 5 4 3 2 1

Moral right of the author has been asserted.

CONTENTS

INTRODUCTION

As kids, all we want is to grow up. We want school, studying and having to do exactly as our parents say to be over. We want freedom and a free hand to make our own decisions. And when all of that does happen and we realize what fools we were to want these things. And so we look back at our school days and reminisce about 'simpler times'. To a certain extent, it holds true; school days were simpler than the complications and responsibilities of adult life. But we often forget how everything we felt in school—as children or teenagers—was immensely intense. And so, when we reach out to school friends, we reach out to people who have helped us navigate the most confusing times of our life.

School is the time we experience some of our firsts—our first friend, first fight, first failure, first success, first love and first heartbreak. We go through it together, with our friends, our classmates, our partners in crime. And this book is a celebration of exactly these emotions. It's a reminder of the joy we felt as children, the simple pleasures in life that make us feel like the kings of the world. A cricket match with a rival school, an unlikely ally that helps you through a lonely time, the many adventures that are encouraged by boyish whims, the curiosity about the wonders of this world—this book is an expedition into our hearts, to ignite the same joy we felt as kids.

Ruskin Bond

BE PREPARED

I was a Boy Scout once, although I couldn't tell a slip knot from a granny knot, nor a reef knot from a thief knot. I did know that a thief knot was to be used to tie up a thief, should you happen to catch one. I have never caught a thief—and wouldn't know what to do with one since I can't tie the right knot. I'd just let him go with a warning, I suppose. And tell him to become a Boy Scout.

'Be prepared!' That's the Boy Scout motto. And it is a good one, too. But I never seem to be well prepared for anything, be it an exam or a journey or the roof blowing off my room. I get halfway through a speech and then forget what I have to say next. Or I make a new suit to attend a friend's wedding, and then turn up in my pyjamas.

So, how did I, the most impractical of boys, survive as a Boy Scout?

Well, it seems a rumour had gone around the junior school (I was still a junior then) that I was a good cook. I had never cooked anything in my life, but of course I had spent a lot of time in the tuck shop making suggestions and advising Chimpu, who ran the tuck shop, and encouraging him to make more and better samosas, jalebies, tikkees and pakoras. For my unwanted advice, he would favour me with an occasional free samosa. So, naturally, I looked upon him as a friend and benefactor. With this qualification, I was given a cookery badge and put in charge of our troop's supply of rations.

There were about twenty of us in our troop. During the summer break, our Scoutmaster, Mr Oliver, took us on a camping expedition to Taradevi, a temple-crowned mountain a few miles outside Shimla. That first night we were put to work, peeling potatoes, skinning onions, shelling peas and pounding masalas. These various ingredients being ready, I was asked, as the troop cookery expert, what should be done with them.

'Put everything in that big degchi,' I ordered. 'Pour half a tin of ghee over the lot. Add some nettle leaves, and cook for half an hour.'

When this was done, everyone had a taste, but the general opinion was that the dish lacked something. 'More salt,' I suggested.

More salt was added. It still lacked something. 'Add a cup of sugar,' I ordered.

Sugar was added to the concoction, but it still lacked something.

'We forgot to add tomatoes,' said one of the Scouts.

'Never mind,' I said. 'We have tomato sauce. Add a bottle of tomato sauce!'

'How about some vinegar?' suggested another boy.

'Just the thing,' I said. 'Add a cup of vinegar!'

'Now it's too sour,' said one of the tasters.

'What jam did we bring?' I asked.

'Gooseberry jam.'

'Just the thing. Empty the bottle!'

The dish was a great success. Everyone enjoyed it, including Mr Oliver, who had no idea what had gone into it.

'What's this called?' he asked.

'It's an all-Indian sweet-and-sour jam-potato curry,' I ventured.

'For short, just call it Bond bhujjia,' said one of the boys. I had earned my cookery badge!

Poor Mr Oliver; he wasn't really cut out to be a Scoutmaster, any more than I was meant to be a Scout.

The following day, he told us he would give us a lesson in tracking. Taking a half-hour start, he walked into the forest, leaving behind him a trail of broken twigs, chicken feathers, pine cones and chestnuts. We were to follow the trail until we found him.

Unfortunately, we were not very good trackers. We did follow Mr Oliver's trail some way into the forest, but then we were distracted by a pool of clear water. It looked very inviting. Abandoning our uniforms, we jumped into the pool and had a great time romping about or just lying on its grassy banks and enjoying the sunshine. Many hours later, feeling hungry, we returned to our campsite and set about preparing the evening meal. It was Bond bhujjia again, but with a few variations.

It was growing dark, and we were beginning to worry about Mr Oliver's whereabouts when he limped into the camp, assisted by a couple of local villagers. Having waited for us at the far end of the forest for a couple of hours, he had decided to return by following his own trail, but in the gathering gloom he was soon lost. Village folk, returning home from the temple, took charge and escorted him back to the camp. He was very angry and made us return all our good-conduct and other badges, which he stuffed into his haversack. I had to give up my cookery badge.

An hour later, when we were all preparing to get into our sleeping bags for the night, Mr Oliver called out, 'Where's dinner?'

'We've had ours,' said one of the boys. 'Everything is finished, sir.'

'Where's Bond? He's supposed to be the cook. Bond, get up and make me an omelette.'

'I can't, sir.'

'Why not?'

'You have my badge. Not allowed to cook without it. Scout rule, sir.'

'I've never heard of such a rule. But you can take your badges, all of you. We return to school tomorrow.'

Mr Oliver returned to his tent in a huff.

But I relented and made him a grand omelette, garnishing it with dandelion leaves and a chilli.

'Never had such an omelette before,' confessed Mr Oliver.

'Would you like another, sir?'

'Tomorrow, Bond, tomorrow. We'll breakfast early tomorrow.'

But we had to break up our camp before we could do that because in the early hours of the next morning, a bear strayed into our camp, entered the tent where our stores were kept, and created havoc with all our provisions, even rolling our biggest degchi down the hillside.

In the confusion and uproar that followed, the bear entered Mr Oliver's tent (our Scoutmaster was already outside, fortunately) and came out entangled in his dressing gown. It then made off towards the forest, a comical sight in its borrowed clothes.

And though we were a troop of brave little scouts, we thought it better to let the bear keep the gown.

THE FOUR FEATHERS

O ur school dormitory was a very long room with about thirty beds, fifteen on either side of the room. This was good for pillow fights. Class V would take on Class VI (the two senior classes in our Prep school) and there would be plenty of space for leaping, struggling small boys, pillows flying, feathers flying, until there was a cry of 'Here comes Fishy!' or 'Here comes Olly!' and either Mr Fisher, the Headmaster, or Mr Oliver, the Senior Master, would come striding in, cane in hand, to put an end to the general mayhem. Pillow fights were allowed, up to a point; nobody got hurt. But parents sometimes complained if, at the end of the term, a boy came home with a pillow devoid of cotton-wool or feathers.

In that last year at Prep school in Shimla, there were four of us who were close friends—Bimal, whose home was in Bombay; Riaz, who came from Lahore; Bran, who hailed from Vellore; and your narrator, who lived wherever his father (then in the Air Force) was posted.

We called ourselves the 'Four Feathers', the feathers

signifying that we were companions in adventure, comrades-in-arms, and knights of the round table. Bimal adopted a peacock's feather as his emblem—he was always a bit showy. Riaz chose a falcon's feather—although we couldn't find one. Bran and I were at first offered crows or murghi feathers, but we protested vigorously and threatened a walkout. Finally, I settled for a parrot's feather (taken from Mrs Fisher's pet parrot), and Bran found a woodpecker's, which suited him, as he was always knocking things about.

Bimal was all thin legs and arms, so light and frisky that at times he seemed to be walking on air. We called him 'Bambi', after the delicate little deer in the Disney film. Riaz, on the other hand, was a sturdy boy, good at games though not very studious; but always good-natured, always smiling.

Bran was a dark, good-looking boy from the South; he was just a little spoilt—hated being given out in a cricket match and would refuse to leave the crease!—but he was affectionate and a loyal friend. I was the 'scribe'—good at inventing stories in order to get out of scrapes—but hopeless at sums, my highest marks being twenty-two out of one hundred.

On Sunday afternoons, when there were no classes or organized games, we were allowed to roam about on the hillside below the school. The Four Feathers would laze about on the short summer grass, sharing the occasional food parcel from home, reading comics (sometimes a book), and making plans for the long winter holidays. My father, who collected everything from stamps to seashells to butterflies, had given me a butterfly net and urged me to try and catch a rare species which, he said, was found only near Chotta Shimla. He described it as a large purple butterfly with yellow and black borders on its wings. A Purple Emperor, I think it was called. As I wasn't very good at identifying butterflies, I would chase anything that happened to flit across the school grounds, usually ending up with Common Red Admirals, Clouded Yellows, or Cabbage Whites. But that Purple Emperor—that rare specimen being sought by collectors the world over—proved elusive. I would have to seek my fortune in some other line of endeavour.

One day, scrambling about among the rocks, and thorny bushes below the school, I almost fell over a small bundle lying in the shade of a young spruce tree. On taking a closer look, I discovered that the bundle was really a baby, wrapped up in a tattered old blanket.

'Feathers, feathers!' I called, 'come here and look. A baby's been left here!'

The feathers joined me and we all stared down at the infant, who was fast asleep.

'Who would leave a baby on the hillside?' asked Bimal of no one in particular.

'Someone who doesn't want it,' said Bran.

'And hoped some good people would come along and keep it,' said Riaz.

'A panther might have come along instead,' I said. 'Can't leave it here.'

'Well, we'll just have to adopt it,' said Bimal.

'We can't adopt a baby,' said Bran.

'Why not?'

'We have to be married.'

'We don't.'

'Not us, you dope. The grown-ups who adopt babies.'

Well, we can't just leave it here for grown-ups to come along,' I said.

'We don't even know if it's a boy or a girl,' said Riaz.

'Makes no difference. A baby's a baby. Let's take it back to school.'

'And keep it in the dormitory?'

'Of course not. Who's going to feed it? Babies need milk. We'll hand it over to Mrs Fisher. She doesn't have a baby.'

'Maybe she doesn't want one. Look, it's beginning to cry. Let's hurry!'

Riaz picked up the wide-awake and crying baby and gave it to Bimal who gave it to Bran who gave it to me. The Four Feathers marched up the hill to school with a very noisy baby.

'Now it's done potty in the blanket,' I complained. 'And some of it's on my shirt.'

'Never mind,' said Bimal. 'It's in a good cause. You're a Boy Scout, remember? You're supposed to help people in distress.'

The headmaster and his wife were in their drawing room, enjoying their afternoon tea and cakes. We trudged in, and Bimal announced, 'We've got something for Mrs Fisher.'

Mrs Fisher took one look at the bundle in my arms and let out a shriek. 'What have you brought here, Bond?'

'A baby, ma'am. I think it's a girl. Do you want to adopt it?'

Mrs Fisher threw up her arms in consternation, and turned to her husband. 'What are we to do, Frank? These boys are impossible. They've picked up someone's child!'

'We'll have to inform the police,' said Mr Fisher, reaching for the telephone. 'We can't have lost babies in the school.'

Just then there was a commotion outside, and a wild-eyed woman, her clothes dishevelled, entered at the front door accompanied by several menfolk from one of the villages. She ran towards us, crying out, 'My baby, my baby! Mera bachcha! You've stolen my baby!'

'We found it on the hillside,' I stammered.

'That's right,' said Bran. 'Finder's keepers!'

'Quiet, Adams,' said Mr Fisher, holding up his hand for order and addressing the villagers in a friendly manner. 'These boys found the baby alone on the hillside and brought it here before…before…'

'Before the hyenas got it,' I put in.

'Quite right, Bond. And why did you leave your child alone?' he asked the woman.

'I put her down for five minutes so that I could climb the plum tree and collect the plums. When I came down, the baby had gone! But I could hear it crying up on the hill. I called the menfolk and we come looking for it.'

'Well, here's your baby,' I said, thrusting it into her arms. By then I was glad to be rid of it! 'Look after it properly in future.'

'Kidnapper!' she screamed at me.

Mr Fisher succeeded in mollifying the villagers. 'These boys are good Scouts,' he told them. 'It's their business to help people.'

'Scout Law Number Three, sir,' I added. 'To be useful and helpful.'

And then the Headmaster turned the tables on the villagers. 'By the way, those plum trees belong to the school. So do the peaches and apricots. Now I know why they've been disappearing so fast!'

The villagers, a little chastened, went their way.

Mr Fisher reached for his cane. From the way he fondled it I knew he was itching to use it on our bottoms.

'No, Frank,' said Mrs Fisher, intervening on our behalf. 'It was really very sweet of them to look after that baby. And look at Bond—he's got baby-goo all over his clothes.'

'So he has. Go and take a bath, all of you. And what are you grinning about, Bond?'

'Scout Law Number Eight, sir. A Scout smiles and whistles under all difficulties.'

And so ended the first adventure of the Four Feathers.

MISS BABCOCK'S BIG TOE

If two people are thrown together for a long time, they can become either close friends or sworn enemies. Thus, it was with Tata and me when we both went down with mumps and had to spend a fortnight together in the school hospital. It wasn't really a hospital—just a five-bed ward in a small cottage on the approach road to our prep-school in Chhota Shimla. It was supervised by a retired nurse, an elderly matron called Miss Babcock, who was all but stone deaf.

Miss Babcock was an able nurse, but she was a fidgety, fussy person, always dashing about from ward to dispensary and to her own room, as a result the boys called her Miss Shuttlecock. As she couldn't hear us, she didn't mind. But her hearing difficulty did create something of a problem, both for her and for her patients. If someone in the ward felt ill late at night, he had to shout or ring a bell, and she heard neither. So, someone had to get up and fetch her.

Miss Babcock devised an ingenious method of waking her in an emergency. She tied a long piece of string to the foot of the sick person's bed; then took the other end of the string to her own room, where, upon retiring for the night, she tied it to her big toe.

A vigorous pull on the string from the sick person, and Miss Babcock would be wide awake!

Now, what could be more tempting to a small boy than— such a device? The string was tied to the foot of Tata's bed, and he was a restless fellow, always wanting water, always complaining of aches and pains. And sometimes, out of plain mischief, he would give several tugs on that string until Miss Babcock arrived with a pill or a glass of water.

'You'll have my toe off by morning,' she complained. 'You don't have to pull quite so hard.'

And what was worse, when Tata did fall asleep, he snored to high heaven and nothing could wake him! I had to lie awake most of the night, listening to his rhythmic snoring. It was like a trumpet tuning up or a bullfrog calling to its mates.

Fortunately, a couple of nights later, we were joined in the ward by Bimal, a friend and fellow 'feather', who had also contracted mumps. One night of Tata's snoring, and Bimal resolved to do something about it.

'Wait until he's fast asleep,' said Bimal, 'and then we'll carry his bed outside and leave him in the veranda.' We did more than that. As Tata commenced his nightly imitation of all the wind instruments in the London Philharmonic Orchestra, we lifted up his bed as gently as possible and carried it out into the garden, putting it down beneath the nearest pine tree.

'It's healthier outside,' said Bimal, justifying our action. 'All this fresh air should cure him.' Leaving Tata to serenade the stars, we returned to the ward expecting to enjoy a good night's sleep. So did Miss Babcock.

However, we couldn't sleep long. We were woken by Miss Babcock running around the ward screaming, 'Where's Tata? Where's Tata?' She ran outside, and we followed dutifully, barefoot, in our pyjamas.

The bed stood where we had put it down, but of Tata, there was no sign. Instead, there was a large black-faced langur at the foot of the bed, baring its teeth in a grin of disfavour.

'Tata's gone,' gasped Miss Babcock.

'He must be a sleepwalker.' said Bimal.

'Maybe the leopard took him,' I said. Just then there was a commotion in the shrubbery at the end of the garden and shouting, 'Help, help!' Tata emerged from the bushes, followed by several lithe, long-tailed langurs, merrily giving chase. Apparently, he'd woken up at the crack of dawn to find his bed surrounded by a gang of inquisitive simians. They had meant no harm, but Tata had panicked, and made a dash for life and liberty, running into the forest instead of into the cottage. We got Tata and his bed back into the ward, and Miss Babcock took his temperature and gave him a dose of salts. Oddly enough, in all the excitement no one asked how Tata and his bed had travelled in the night.

And strangely, he did not snore the following night; so perhaps the pine-scented night air really helped. Needless to say, we all soon recovered from the mumps, and Miss Babcock's big toe received a well-deserved rest.

SOMETIMES SCHOOL WAS FUN

Schooldays were not always fun, but there were times when I did enjoy being at boarding school, and I think the good times outweighed the tedium of day-to-day school routine.

Acting in school plays was probably the greatest fun. Even rehearsals were fun, because they meant escaping that hour of compulsory evening study, or staying up a little later than usual after supper. I was quite a good little actor, and was usually given 'character' parts, such as a drunken sailor or a comical farmhand. I enjoyed these roles and would often keep the boys in our dormitory awake by belting out my favourite song:

Oh, what shall we do with a drunken sailor,
Early in the morning?
Put him in a tub and wet him all over,
Early in the morning!

The rest of the dormitory would threaten to wet me all over if I did not shut up, but I was quite capable of looking after myself.

The play was called *Borrowed Plumes*. It was a one-act farce, and in it I had to put on a Cockney accent and spend a lot of time gulping down 'whisky' from a liquor bottle. The whisky was, in fact, just plain tea, without milk or sugar, and after three evenings of swallowing the stuff, I resolved never to touch tea again!

For the part, I had also to wear a false beard. The teacher who was in charge of make-up did not stick it on properly, with the result that for most of the final performance I kept making frantic efforts to keep my beard from falling off. The audience thought that was part of the play, and I was voted the best actor for playing the role so naturally.

What else did I enjoy at school?

I did not care for races, long or short, but I played field games such as hockey, football and cricket.

I did attempt to get into the school cricket eleven, but for some strange reason I was always made the 'twelfth man' and had to carry out the drinks or do the fielding whenever one of the star batsmen was indisposed. But I had my revenge. During an inter-school match when I was left in charge of the refreshments in the pavilion, I quietly polished off all the chicken sandwiches. When the players came in for tea, they had to make do with tomato sandwiches.

After that, I wasn't even considered for that job.

But I did excel at football and held my place as goalkeeper for three years. Nobody else wanted to scrape the skin off their knees and elbows on the stony Shimla playing fields.

I have mentioned my aversion to races and to athletics in general, having once almost decapitated my housemaster with a wild discus throw. The marathon was worst of all, as it involved a five-mile slog from the Viceregal Lodge to Chotta Shimla. I generally came in last, not so much because of my lethargic pace (it was that too), but because I had discovered a little by-lane along the route where an enterprising gentleman made tikkees and samosas. I would stop here for a bite—or rather several bites—before making a valiant attempt to catch up with the others. Sometimes I did catch up with them, the refreshment having given me an extra boost of energy.

My favourite place was, of course, the school library. And a far-seeing senior master, Mr Knight, put me in charge of the library and left the keys with me. After class hours, or whenever I was free, I would slip into the library and sit amongst these hundreds of books, reading them, arranging them, cataloguing them, or just being with them. Here I made many life-long friends. And sometimes in the evening, when twilight filled the room, the gentle ghosts of Dickens, Barrie, Stevenson and others would emerge from the bookshelves, and gaze tolerantly at the boy who sat alone near the window, dreaming of becoming a writer.

HERE COMES MR OLIVER

Apart from being our Scoutmaster, Mr Oliver taught us maths, a subject in which I had some difficulty obtaining pass marks. Sometimes I scraped through; usually I got something like twenty or thirty out of a hundred. 'Failed again, Bond,' Mr Oliver would say. 'What will you do when you grow up?' 'Become a scoutmaster, sir.'

'Scoutmasters don't get paid. It's an honorary job. You could become a cook. That would suit you.' He hadn't forgotten our Scout camp, when I had been the camp's cook.

If Mr Oliver was in a good mood, he'd give me grace marks, passing me by a mark or two. He wasn't a hard man, but he seldom smiled. He was very dark, thin, stooped (from a distance he looked like a question mark), and balding. He was about forty, still a bachelor, and it was said that he had been unlucky in love—that the girl he was going to marry jilted him at the last moment, running away with a sailor while Mr Oliver waited at the church, ready for the wedding ceremony. No wonder he always had such a sorrowful look.

·

Mr Oliver did have one inseparable companion: a dachshund, a snappy little 'sausage' of a dog, who looked upon the human race, and especially small boys, with a certain disdain and frequent hostility. We called him Hitler. (This was 1945, and the dictator was at the end of his tether.) He was impervious to overtures of friendship, and if you tried to pat or stroke him he would do his best to bite your fingers or your shin or ankle. However, he was devoted to Mr Oliver and followed him everywhere except into the classroom; this our Headmaster would not allow. You remember that old nursery rhyme:

Mary had a little lamb,
Its fleece was white as snow,
And everywhere that Mary went
The lamb was sure to go.

Well, we made up our own version of the rhyme, and I must confess to having had a hand in its composition. It went like this:

Olly had a little dog,
It was never out of sight,
And everyone that Olly met
The dog was sure to bite!

It followed him about the school grounds. It followed him when he took a walk through the pines to the Brockhuist tennis courts. It followed him into town and home again. Mr Oliver had no other friend, no other companion. The dog slept at the foot of Mr Oliver's bed. It did not sit at the breakfast table, but it had buttered toast for breakfast and soup and crackers for dinner. Mr Oliver had to take his lunch in the dining hall with the staff and boys, but he had an arrangement with one of the bearers whereby a plate of dal, rice and chapattis made its way to Mr Oliver's quarters and his well-fed pet.

And then tragedy struck.

Mr Oliver and Hitler were returning to school after an evening walk through the pines. It was dusk, and the light was fading fast. Out of the shadows of the trees emerged a lean and hungry panther. It pounced on the hapless dog, flung it across the road, seized it between its powerful jaws, and made off with its victim into the darkness of the forest.

Mr Oliver was untouched but frozen into immobility for at least a minute. Then he began calling for help. Some bystanders, who had witnessed the incident, began shouting too. Mr Oliver ran into the forest, but there was no sign of the dog or the panther.

Mr Oliver appeared to be a broken man. He went about his duties with a poker face, but we could all tell that he was grieving for his lost companion, for in the classroom he was listless and indifferent to whether or not we followed his calculations on the blackboard. In times of personal loss, the Highest Common Factor made no sense.

Mr Oliver was no longer seen going on his evening walk. He stayed in his room, playing cards with himself. He played with his food, pushing most of it aside. There were no chapattis to send home.

'Olly needs another pet,' said Bimal, wise in the ways of adults.

'Or a wife,' said Tata, who thought on those lines.

'He's too old. He must be over forty.'

'A pet is best,' I said. 'What about a parrot?'

'You can't take a parrot for a walk,' said Bimal. 'Olly wants someone to walk beside him.'

'A cat maybe.'

'Hitler hated cats. A cat would be an insult to Hitler's memory.'

'Then he needs another dachshund. But there aren't any around here.'

'Any dog will do. We'll ask Chimpu to get us a pup.'

Chimpu ran the tuck shop. He lived in the Chotta Shimla bazaar, and occasionally we would ask him to bring us tops or marbles, a corflic or other little things that we couldn't get in school. Five of us Boy Scouts contributed a rupee each, which we gave to Chimpu and asked him to get us a pup. 'A good breed,' we told him, 'not a mongrel.'

The next evening Chimpu turned up with a pup that seemed to be a combination of at least five different breeds, all good ones no doubt. One ear lay flat, the other stood upright. It was spotted like a Dalmatian, but it had the legs of a spaniel and the tail of a Pomeranian. It was floppy and playful, and the tail wagged a lot, which was more than Hitler's ever did.

'It's quite pretty,' said Tata. 'Must be a female.'

'He may not want a female,' said Bimal.

'Let's give it a try,' I said.

'During our play hour, before the bell rang for supper, we left the pup on the steps outside Mr Oliver's front door. Then we knocked, and sped into the hibiscus bush that lined the pathway.

Mr Oliver opened the door. He looked down at the pup with an expressionless face. The pup began to paw at Mr Oliver's shoes, loosening one of his laces in the process.

'Away with you!' muttered Mr Oliver. 'Buzz off!' And he pushed the pup away, gently but firmly, and closed the door.

We went through the same procedure again, but the result was much the same. We now had a playful pup on our hands, and Chimpu had gone home for the night. We would have to conceal it in the dormitory.

At first we hid it in Bimal's locker, but it began to yelp and struggled to get out. Tata took it into the shower room, but it wouldn't stay there either. It began running around the dormitory, playing with socks, shoes, slippers, and anything else it could get hold of.

'Watch out!' hissed one of the boys. 'Here comes Fisher!'

Mrs Fisher, the Headmaster's wife, was on her nightly rounds, checking to make sure we were all in bed and not up to some natural mischief. I grabbed the pup and hid it under my blanket. It was quiet there, happy to nibble at my toes. When Mrs Fisher had gone, I let the pup loose again, and for the rest of the night it had the freedom of the dormitory.

At the crack of dawn, before first light, Bimal and I sped out of the dormitory in our pyjamas, taking the pup with us. We banged hard on Mr Oliver's door, and kept knocking until we heard footsteps approaching. As soon as the door was slowly opened, we pushed the pup inside and ran for our lives.

Mr Oliver came to class as usual, but there was no pup with him. Three or four days passed, and still no sign of the pup! Had he passed it on to someone else, or simply let it wander off on its own?

'Here comes Olly!' called Bimal, from our vantage point near the school bell.

Mr Oliver was setting out for his evening walk. He was carrying a strong walnut-wood walking stick—to keep panthers at bay, no doubt. He looked neither left nor right, and if he noticed us watching him, Mr Oliver gave no sign. But then, scurrying behind him was the pup! The creature of many good breeds was accompanying Mr Oliver on his walk. It had been well brushed and was wearing a bright red collar. Like Mr Oliver, it took no notice of us. It walked along beside its new master.

Mr Oliver and the little pup were soon inseparable companions, and my friends and I were quite pleased with ourselves. Mr Oliver gave absolutely no indication that he knew where the pup had come from, but when the end-of-term exams were over, and Bimal and I were sure that we had failed our maths papers, we were surprised to find that we had passed after all—with grace marks!

'Good old Olly!' said Bimal. 'So he knew all the time.' Tata, of course, did not need grace marks—he was a wizard at maths—but Bimal and I decided we would thank Mr Oliver for his kindness.

'Nothing to thank me for,' said Mr Oliver gruffly, but with a twist at the corners of his mouth, which was the nearest he came to a smile. 'I've seen enough of you two in junior school. It's high time you went up to the senior school—and God help you there!'

THE WHISTLING SCHOOLBOY

The moon was almost at the full. Bright moonlight flooded the road. But I was stalked by the shadows of the trees, by the crooked oak branches reaching out towards me—some threateningly, others as though they needed companionship.

Once I dreamt that the trees could walk. That on moonlit nights like this they would uproot themselves for a while, visit each other, talk about old times—for they had seen many men and happenings, especially the older ones. And then, before dawn, they would return to the places where they had been condemned to grow. Lonely sentinels of the night. And this was a good night for them to walk. They appeared eager to do so: a restless rustling of leaves, the creaking of branches—these were sounds that came from within them in the silence of the night.

Occasionally other strollers passed me in the dark. It was still quite early, just eight o'clock, and some people were on their way home. Others were walking into town for a taste of the bright lights, shops and restaurants. On the unlit road I could not recognize them. They did not notice me. I was reminded of an old song from my childhood. Softly, I began humming the tune, and soon the words came back to me:

We three,
We're not a crowd;
We're not even company—
My echo,
My shadow,
And me...

I looked down at my shadow, moving silently beside me. We take our shadows for granted, don't we? There they are, the uncomplaining companions of a lifetime, mute and helpless witnesses to our every act of commission or omission. On this bright moonlit night I could not help noticing you, Shadow, and I was sorry that you had to see so much that I was ashamed of; but glad, too, that you were around when I had my small triumphs. And what of my echo? I thought of calling out to see if my call came back to me; but I refrained from doing so, as I did not wish to disturb the perfect stillness of the mountains or the conversations of the trees.

The road wound up the hill and levelled out at the top, where it became a ribbon of moonlight entwined between tall deodars. A flying squirrel glided across the road, leaving one tree for another. A nightjar called. The rest was silence.

The old cemetery loomed up before me. There were many old graves—some large and monumental—and there were a few recent graves too, for the cemetery was still in use. I could see flowers scattered on one of them—a few late dahlias and scarlet salvia. Further on near the boundary wall, part of the cemetery's retaining wall had collapsed in the heavy monsoon rains. Some of the tombstones had come down with the wall.

One grave lay exposed. A rotting coffin and a few scattered bones were the only relics of someone who had lived and loved like you and me.

Part of the tombstone lay beside the road, but the lettering had worn away. I am not normally a morbid person, but something made me stoop and pick up a smooth round shard of bone, probably part of a skull. When my hand closed over it, the bone crumbled into fragments. I let them fall to the grass. Dust to dust. And from somewhere, not too far away, came the sound of someone whistling.

At first I thought it was another late-evening stroller, whistling to himself much as I had been humming my old song. But the whistler approached quite rapidly; the whistling was loud and cheerful. A boy on a bicycle sped past. I had only a glimpse of him, before his cycle went weaving through the shadows on the road.

But he was back again in a few minutes. And this time he stopped a few feet away from me, and gave me a quizzical half-smile. A slim dusky boy of fourteen or fifteen. He wore a school blazer and a yellow scarf. His eyes were pools of liquid moonlight.

'You don't have a bell on your cycle,' I said.

He said nothing, just smiled at me with his head a little to one side. I put out my hand, and I thought he was going to take it. But then, quite suddenly, he was off again, whistling cheerfully though rather tunelessly. A whistling schoolboy. A bit late for him to be out but he seemed an independent sort.

The whistling grew fainter, then faded away altogether. A deep sound-denying silence fell upon the forest. My shadow and I walked home.

Next morning I woke to a different kind of whistling—the

song of the thrush outside my window.

It was a wonderful day, the sunshine warm and sensuous, and I longed to be out in the open. But there was work to be done, proofs to be corrected, letters to be written. And it was several days before I could walk to the top of the hill, to that lonely tranquil resting place under the deodars. It seemed to me ironic that those who had the best view of the glistening snow-capped peaks were all buried several feet underground.

Some repair work was going on. The retaining wall of the cemetery was being shored up, but the overseer told me that there was no money to restore the damaged grave. With the help of the chowkidar, I returned the scattered bones to a little hollow under the collapsed masonry, and left some money with him so that he could have the open grave bricked up. The name on the gravestone had worn away, but I could make out a date—20 November 1950—some fifty years ago, but not too long ago as gravestones go.

I found the burial register in the church vestry and turned back the yellowing pages to 1950, when I was just a schoolboy myself. I found the name there—Michael Dutta, aged fifteen—and the cause of death: road accident.

Well, I could only make guesses. And to turn conjecture into certainty, I would have to find an old resident who might remember the boy or the accident.

There was old Miss Marley at Pine Top. A retired teacher from Woodstock, she had a wonderful memory, and had lived in the hill station for more than half a century.

White-haired and smooth-cheeked, her bright blue eyes full of curiosity, she *gazed* benignly at me through her old-fashioned pince-nez.

'Michael was a charming boy—full of exuberance, always

ready to oblige. I had only to mention that I needed a newspaper or an Aspirin, and he'd be off on his bicycle, swooping down these steep roads with great abandon. But these hills roads, with their sudden corners, weren't meant for racing around on a bicycle. They were widening our roads for motor traffic, and a truck was coming uphill, loaded with rubble, when Michael came round a bend and smashed headlong into it. He was rushed to the hospital, and the doctors did their best, but he did not recover consciousness. Of course, you must have seen his grave. That's why you're here. His parents? They left shortly afterwards. Went abroad, I think…A charming boy, Michael, but just a bit too reckless. You'd have liked him, I think.'

I did not see the phantom bicycle rider again for some time, although I felt his presence on more than one occasion. And when, on a cold winter's evening, I walked past that lonely cemetery, I thought I heard him whistling far away. But he did not manifest himself. Perhaps it was only the echo of a whistle, in communion with my insubstantial shadow.

It was several months before I saw that smiling face again. And then it came at me out of the mist as I was walking home in drenching monsoon rain. I had been to a dinner party at the old community centre, and I was returning home along a very narrow, precipitous path known as the Eyebrow. A storm had been threatening all evening. A heavy mist had settled on the hillside. It was so thick that the light from my torch simply bounced off it. The sky blossomed with sheet lightning and thunder rolled over the mountains. The rain became heavier. I moved forward slowly, carefully, hugging the hillside. There was a clap of thunder, and then I saw him emerge from the mist and stand in my way—the same slim dark youth who had materialized near the cemetery. He did not smile. Instead he put up his hand and waved at me. I hesitated, stood still. The mist lifted a little, and I saw that the path had disappeared. There was a gaping emptiness a few feet in front of me. And then a drop of over a hundred feet to the rocks below.

As I stepped back, clinging to a thorn bush for support, the boy vanished. I stumbled back to the community centre and spent the night on a chair in the library.

I did not see him again.

But weeks later, when I was down with a severe bout of flu, I heard him from my sickbed, whistling beneath my window. *Was he calling to me to join him*, I wondered, *or was he just trying to reassure me that all was well?* I got out of bed and looked out, but I saw no one. From time to time I heard his whistling; but as I got better, it grew fainter until it ceased altogether.

Fully recovered, I renewed my old walks to the top of the hill. But although I lingered near the cemetery until it grew dark, and paced up and down the deserted road, I did not see or hear the whistler again. I felt lonely, in need of a friend, even if it was only a phantom bicycle rider. But there were only the trees.

And so every evening I walk home in the darkness, singing the old refrain:

We three,
We're not alone,
We're not even company—
My echo,
My shadow,
And me...

THE SCHOOL AMONG THE PINES

1

A leopard, lithe and sinewy, drank at the mountain stream, and then lay down on the grass to bask in the late February sunshine. Its tail twitched occasionally and the animal appeared to be sleeping. At the sound of distant voices it raised its head to listen, then stood up and leapt lightly over the boulders in the stream, disappearing among the trees on the opposite bank.

A minute or two later, three children came walking down the forest path. They were a girl and two boys, and they were singing in their local dialect an old song they had learnt from their grandparents.

Five more miles to go!
We climb through rain and snow.
A river to cross...
A mountain to pass...
Now we've four more miles to go!

Their school satchels looked new, their clothes had been washed and pressed. Their loud and cheerful singing startled a Spotted Forktail. The bird left its favourite rock in the stream and flew down the dark ravine.

'Well, we have only three more miles to go,' said the bigger boy, Prakash, who had been this way hundreds of times. 'But first we have to cross the stream.'

He was a sturdy twelve-year-old with eyes like raspberries and a mop of bushy hair that refused to settle down on his head. The girl and her small brother were taking this path for the first time.

'I'm feeling tired, Bina,' said the little boy.

Bina smiled at him, and Prakash said, 'Don't worry, Sonu, you'll get used to the walk. There's plenty of time.' He glanced at the old watch he'd been given by his grandfather. It needed constant winding. 'We can rest here for five or six minutes.'

They sat down on a smooth boulder and watched the clear water of the shallow stream tumbling downhill. Bina examined the old watch on Prakash's wrist. The glass was badly scratched and she could barely make out the figures on the dial. 'Are you sure it still gives the right time?' she asked.

'Well, it loses five minutes every day, so I put it ten minutes forward at night. That means by morning it's quite accurate! Even our teacher, Mr Mani, asks me for the time. If he doesn't ask, I tell him! The clock in our classroom keeps stopping.'

They removed their shoes and let the cold mountain water run over their feet. Bina was the same age as Prakash. She had pink cheeks, soft brown eyes, and hair that was just beginning to lose its natural curls. Hers was a gentle face, but a determined little chin showed that she could be a strong person. Sonu, her younger brother, was ten. He was a thin boy who had been sickly as a child but was now beginning to fill out. Although he did not look very athletic, he could run like the wind.

Bina had been going to school in her own village of Koli, on the other side of the mountain. But it had been a primary school, finishing at Class Five. Now, in order to study in the Sixth, she would have to walk several miles every day to Nauti, where there was a high school going up to the Eighth. It had been decided that Sonu would also shift to the new school, to give Bina company. Prakash, their neighbour in Koli, was already a pupil at the Nauti school. His mischievous nature, which sometimes got him into trouble, had resulted in his having to repeat a year.

But this didn't seem to bother him. 'What's the hurry?' he had told his indignant parents. 'You're not sending me to a foreign land when I finish school. And our cows aren't running away, are they?'

'You would prefer to look after the cows, wouldn't you?' asked Bina, as they got up to continue their walk.

'Oh, school's all right. Wait till you see old Mr Mani. He always gets our names mixed up, as well as the subjects he's supposed to be teaching. At our last lesson, instead of maths, he gave us a geography lesson!'

'More fun than maths,' said Bina.

'Yes, but there's a new teacher this year. She's very young, they say, just out of college. I wonder what she'll be like.'

Bina walked faster and Sonu had some trouble keeping up with them. She was excited about the new school and the prospect of different surroundings. She had seldom been outside her own village, with its small school and single ration shop. The day's routine never varied—helping her mother in the fields or with household tasks like fetching water from the spring or cutting grass and fodder for the cattle. Her father, who was a soldier, was away for nine months in the year and Sonu was still too small for the heavier tasks.

As they neared Nauti village, they were joined by other children coming from different directions. Even where there were no major roads, the mountains were full of little lanes and short cuts. Like a game of snakes and ladders, these narrow paths zigzagged around the hills and villages, cutting through fields and crossing narrow ravines until they came together to form a fairly busy road along which mules, cattle and goats joined the throng.

Nauti was a fairly large village, and from here a broader but dustier road started for Tehri. There was a small bus, several trucks and (for part of the way) a road-roller. The road hadn't been completed because the heavy diesel roller couldn't take the steep climb to Nauti. It stood on the roadside half way up the road from Tehri.

Prakash knew almost everyone in the area, and exchanged greetings and gossip with other children as well as with muleteers, bus drivers, milkmen and labourers working on the road. He loved telling everyone the time, even if they weren't interested.

'It's nine o'clock,' he would announce, glancing at his wrist. 'Isn't your bus leaving today?'

'Off with you!' the bus driver would respond, 'I'll leave when I'm ready.'

As the children approached Nauti, the small flat school buildings came into view on the outskirts of the village, fringed with a line of long-leaved pines. A small crowd had assembled on the playing field. Something unusual seemed to have happened. Prakash ran forward to see what it was all about. Bina and Sonu stood aside, waiting in a patch of sunlight near the boundary wall.

Prakash soon came running back to them. He was bubbling

over with excitement.

'It's Mr Mani!' he gasped. 'He's disappeared! People are saying a leopard must have carried him off!'

2

Mr Mani wasn't really old. He was about fifty-five and was expected to retire soon. But for the children, adults over forty seemed ancient! And Mr Mani had always been a bit absent-minded, even as a young man.

He had gone out for his early morning walk, saying he'd be back by eight o'clock, in time to have his breakfast and be ready for class. He wasn't married, but his sister and her husband stayed with him. When it was past nine o'clock his sister presumed he'd stopped at a neighbour's house for breakfast (he loved tucking into other people's breakfast) and that he had gone on to school from there. But when the school bell rang at ten o'clock, and everyone but Mr Mani was present, questions were asked and guesses were made.

No one had seen him return from his walk and enquiries made in the village showed that he had not stopped at anyone's house. For Mr Mani to disappear was puzzling; for him to disappear without his breakfast was extraordinary.

Then a milkman returning from the next village said he had seen a leopard sitting on a rock on the outskirts of the pine forest. There had been talk of a cattle-killer in the valley, of leopards and other animals being displaced by the construction of a dam. But as yet no one had heard of a leopard attacking a man. Could Mr Mani have been its first victim? Someone found a strip of red cloth entangled in a blackberry bush and went running through the village showing it to everyone. Mr

Mani had been known to wear red pyjamas. Surely, he had been seized and eaten! But where were his remains? And why had he been in his pyjamas?

Meanwhile, Bina and Sonu and the rest of the children had followed their teachers into the school playground. Feeling a little lost, Bina looked around for Prakash. She found herself facing a dark slender young woman wearing spectacles, who must have been in her early twenties—just a little too old to be another student. She had a kind expressive face and she seemed a little concerned by all that had been happening.

Bina noticed that she had lovely hands; it was obvious that the new teacher hadn't milked cows or worked in the fields!

'You must be new here,' said the teacher, smiling at Bina. 'And is this your little brother?'

'Yes, we've come from Koli village. We were at school there.'

'It's a long walk from Koli. You didn't see any leopards, did you? Well, I'm new too. Are you in the Sixth class?'

'Sonu is in the Third. I'm in the Sixth.'

'Then I'm your new teacher. My name is Tania Ramola. Come along, let's see if we can settle down in our classroom.'

Mr Mani turned up at twelve o'clock, wondering what all the fuss was about. No, he snapped, he had not been attacked by a leopard; and yes, he had lost his pyjamas and would someone kindly return them to him?

'How did you lose your pyjamas, sir?' asked Prakash.

'They were blown off the washing line!' snapped Mr Mani.

After much questioning, Mr Mani admitted that he had gone further than he had intended, and that he had lost his way coming back. He had been a bit upset because the new teacher, a slip of a girl, had been given charge of the Sixth, while he was still with the Fifth, along with that troublesome boy Prakash, who kept on reminding him of the time! The headmaster had explained that as Mr Mani was due to retire at the end of the year, the school did not wish to burden him with a senior class. But Mr Mani looked upon the whole thing as a plot to get rid of him. He glowered at Miss Ramola whenever he passed her. And when she smiled back at him, he looked the other way!

Mr Mani had been getting even more absent-minded of late—putting on his shoes without his socks, wearing his homespun waistcoat inside out, mixing up people's names and, of course, eating other people's lunches and dinners. His sister had made a special mutton broth (*pai*) for the postmaster, who was down with flu and had asked Mr Mani to take it over in a thermos. When the postmaster opened the thermos, he found only a few drops of broth at the bottom—Mr Mani had drunk the rest somewhere along the way.

When sometimes Mr Mani spoke of his coming retirement, it was to describe his plans for the small field he owned just behind the house. Right now, it was full of potatoes, which did not require much looking after; but he had plans for growing dahlias, roses, French beans, and other fruits and flowers.

The next time he visited Tehri, he promised himself, he would buy some dahlia bulbs and rose cuttings. The monsoon season would be a good time to put them down. And meanwhile, his potatoes were still flourishing.

3

Bina enjoyed her first day at the new school. She felt at ease with Miss Ramola, as did most of the boys and girls in her class. Tania Ramola had been to distant towns such as Delhi and Lucknow—places they had only read about—and it was said that she had a brother who was a pilot and flew planes all over the world. Perhaps he'd fly over Nauti some day!

Most of the children had, of course, seen planes flying overhead, but none of them had seen a ship, and only a few had been on a train. Tehri mountain was far from the railway and hundreds of miles from the sea. But they all knew about the big dam that was being built at Tehri, just forty miles away.

Bina, Sonu and Prakash had company for part of the way home, but gradually the other children went off in different directions. Once they had crossed the stream, they were on their own again.

It was a steep climb all the way back to their village. Prakash had a supply of peanuts which he shared with Bina and Sonu, and at a small spring they quenched their thirst.

When they were less than a mile from home, they met a postman who had finished his round of the villages in the area and was now returning to Nauti.

'Don't waste time along the way,' he told them. 'Try to get home before dark.'

'What's the hurry?' asked Prakash, glancing at his watch. 'It's only five o'clock.'

'There's a leopard around. I saw it this morning, not far from the stream. No one is sure how it got here. So don't take any chances. Get home early.'

'So there really is a leopard,' said Sonu.

They took his advice and walked faster, and Sonu forgot to complain about his aching feet.

They were home well before sunset.

There was a smell of cooking in the air and they were hungry.

'Cabbage and roti,' said Prakash gloomily. 'But I could eat anything today.' He stopped outside his small slate-roofed house, and Bina and Sonu waved him goodbye, then carried on across a couple of ploughed fields until they reached their small stone house.

'Stuffed tomatoes,' said Sonu, sniffing just outside the front door.

'And lemon pickle,' said Bina, who had helped cut, sun and salt the lemons a month previously.

Their mother was lighting the kitchen stove. They greeted her with great hugs and demands for an immediate dinner. She was a good cook who could make even the simplest of dishes taste delicious. Her favourite saying was, 'Homemade *pai* is better than chicken soup in Delhi,' and Bina and Sonu had to agree.

Electricity had yet to reach their village, and they took their meal by the light of a kerosene lamp. After the meal, Sonu settled down to do a little homework, while Bina stepped outside to look at the stars.

Across the fields, someone was playing a flute. *It must be Prakash*, thought Bina. *He always breaks off on the high notes*. But the flute music was simple and appealing, and she began singing softly to herself in the dark.

4

Mr Mani was having trouble with the porcupines. They had been getting into his garden at night and digging up and eating his potatoes. From his bedroom window—left open, now that the mild-April weather had arrived—he could listen to them enjoying the vegetables he had worked hard to grow. Scrunch, scrunch! *Katar, katar*, as their sharp teeth sliced through the largest and juiciest of potatoes. For Mr Mani it was as though they were biting through his own flesh. And the sound of them digging industriously as they rooted up those healthy, leafy plants, made him tremble with rage and indignation. The unfairness of it all!

Yes, Mr Mani hated porcupines. He prayed for their destruction, their removal from the face of the earth. But, as his friends were quick to point out, 'Bhagwan protected porcupines too,' and in any case you could never see the creatures or catch them, they were completely nocturnal.

Mr Mani got out of bed every night, torch in one hand, a stout stick in the other, but as soon as he stepped into the garden the crunching and digging stopped and he was greeted by the most infuriating of silences. He would grope around in the dark, swinging wildly with the stick, but not a single porcupine was to be seen or heard. As soon as he was back in bed—the sounds would start all over again. Scrunch, scrunch, *katar, katar*...

Mr Mani came to his class tired and dishevelled, with rings beneath his eyes and a permanent frown on his face. It took some time for his pupils to discover the reason for his misery, but when they did, they felt sorry for their teacher and took to discussing ways and means of saving his potatoes from the porcupines.

It was Prakash who came up with the idea of a moat or waterditch. 'Porcupines don't like water,' he said knowledgeably.

'How do you know?' asked one of his friends.

'Throw water on one and see how it runs! They don't like getting their quills wet.'

There was no one who could disprove Prakash's theory, and the class fell in with the idea of building a moat, especially as it meant getting most of the day off.

'Anything to make Mr Mani happy,' said the headmaster, and the rest of the school watched with envy as the pupils of Class Five, armed with spades and shovels collected from all parts of the village, took up their positions around Mr Mani's potato field and began digging a ditch.

By evening the moat was ready, but it was still dry and the porcupines got in again that night and had a great feast.

'At this rate,' said Mr Mani gloomily 'there won't be any potatoes left to save.'

But next day Prakash and the other boys and girls managed to divert the water from a stream that flowed past the village. They had the satisfaction of watching it flow gently into the ditch. Everyone went home in a good mood. By nightfall, the ditch had overflowed, the potato field was flooded, and Mr Mani found himself trapped inside his house. But Prakash and his friends had won the day. The porcupines stayed away that night!

A month had passed, and wild violets, daisies and buttercups now sprinkled the hill slopes, and on her way to school Bina gathered enough to make a little posy. The bunch of flowers fitted easily into an old ink well. Miss Ramola was delighted to find this little display in the middle of her desk.

'Who put these here?' she asked in surprise.

Bina kept quiet, and the rest of the class smiled secretively. After that, they took turns bringing flowers for the classroom.

On her long walks to school and home again, Bina became aware that April was the month of new leaves. The oak leaves were bright green above and silver beneath, and when they rippled in the breeze they were like clouds of silvery green. The path was strewn with old leaves, dry and crackly. Sonu loved kicking them around.

Clouds of white butterflies floated across the stream. Sonu was chasing a butterfly when he stumbled over something dark and repulsive. He went sprawling on the grass. When he got to his feet, he looked down at the remains of a small animal.

'Bina! Prakash! Come quickly!' he shouted.

It was part of a sheep, killed some days earlier by a much larger animal.

'Only a leopard could have done this,' said Prakash.

'Let's get away, then,' said Sonu. 'It might still be around!'

'No, there's nothing left to eat. The leopard will be hunting elsewhere by now. Perhaps it's moved on to the next valley.'

'Still, I'm frightened,' said Sonu. 'There may be more leopards!'

Bina took him by the hand. 'Leopards don't attack humans!' she said.

'They will, if they get a taste for people!' insisted Prakash.

'Well, this one hasn't attacked any people as yet,' said Bina, although she couldn't be sure. Hadn't there been rumours of a leopard attacking some workers near the dam? But she did not want Sonu to feel afraid, so she did not mention the story. All she said was, 'It has probably come here because of all the activity near the dam.'

All the same, they hurried home. And for a few days, whenever they reached the stream, they crossed over very quickly, unwilling to linger too long at that lovely spot.

5

A few days later, a school party was on its way to Tehri to see the new dam that was being built.

Miss Ramola had arranged to take her class, and Mr Mani, not wishing to be left out, insisted on taking his class as well. That meant there were about fifty boys and girls taking part in the outing. The little bus could only take thirty. A friendly truck driver agreed to take some children if they were prepared to sit on sacks of potatoes. And Prakash persuaded the owner of the diesel roller to turn it round and head it back to Tehri—with him and a couple of friends up on the driving seat.

Prakash's small group set off at sunrise, as they had to walk some distance in order to reach the stranded road roller. The bus left at 9 a.m. with Miss Ramola and her class, and Mr Mani and some of his pupils. The truck was to follow later.

It was Bina's first visit to a large town and her first bus ride.

The sharp curves along the winding, downhill road made several children feel sick. The bus driver seemed to be in a tearing hurry. He took them along at rolling, rollicking speed, which made Bina feel quite giddy. She rested her head on her arms and refused to look out of the window. Hairpin bends and cliff edges, pine forests and snowcapped peaks, all swept past her, but she felt too ill to want to look at anything. It was just as well—those sudden drops, hundreds of feet to the valley below, were quite frightening. Bina began to wish that she hadn't come—or that she had joined Prakash on the road roller instead!

Miss Ramola and Mr Mani didn't seem to notice the lurching and groaning of the old bus. They had made this journey many times. They were busy arguing about the advantages and disadvantages of large dams—an argument that was to continue on and off for much of the day; sometimes in Hindi, sometimes in English, sometimes in the local dialect!

Meanwhile, Prakash and his friends had reached the roller. The driver hadn't turned up, but they managed to reverse it and get it going in the direction of Tehri. They were soon overtaken by both the bus and the truck but kept moving along at a steady chug. Prakash spotted Bina at the window of the bus and waved cheerfully. She responded feebly.

Bina felt better when the road levelled out near Tehri. As they crossed an old bridge over the wide river, they were startled by a loud bang which made the bus shudder. A cloud of dust rose above the town.

'They're blasting the mountain,' said Miss Ramola.

'End of a mountain,' said Mr Mani mournfully.

While they were drinking cups of tea at the bus stop, waiting for the potato truck and the road roller, Miss Ramola and Mr Mani continued their argument about the dam. Miss Ramola maintained that it would bring electric power and water for irrigation to large areas of the country, including the surrounding area. Mr Mani declared that it was a menace, as it was situated in an earthquake zone. There would be a terrible disaster if the dam burst! Bina found it all very confusing. *And what about the animals in the area*, she wondered. *What would happen to them?*

The argument was becoming quite heated when the potato truck arrived. There was no sign of the road roller, so it was decided that Mr Mani should wait for Prakash and his friends while Miss Ramola's group went ahead.

Some eight or nine miles before Tehri the road roller had broken down, and Prakash and his friends were forced to walk. They had not gone far, however, when a mule train came along—five or six mules that had been delivering sacks of grain in Nauti. A boy rode on the first mule, but the others had no loads.

'Can you give us a ride to Tehri?' called Prakash.

'Make yourselves comfortable,' said the boy.

There were no saddles, only gunny sacks strapped on to the mules with rope. They had a rough but jolly ride down to the Tehri bus stop. None of them had ever ridden mules; but they had saved at least an hour on the road.

Looking around the bus stop for the rest of the party, they could find no one from their school. And Mr Mani, who should have been waiting for them, had vanished.

6

Tania Ramola and her group had taken the steep road to the hill above Tehri. Half an hour's climbing brought them to a little plateau which overlooked the town, the river and the dam site.

The earthworks for the dam were only just coming up, but a wide tunnel had been bored through the mountain to divert the river into another channel. Down below, the old town was still spread out across the valley and from a distance it looked quite charming and picturesque.

'Will the whole town be swallowed up by the waters of the dam?' asked Bina.

'Yes, all of it,' said Miss Ramola. 'The clock tower and the old palace. The long bazaar, and the temples, the schools and the jail, and hundreds of houses, for many miles up the valley. All those people will have to go—thousands of them! Of course, they'll be resettled elsewhere.'

'But the town's been here for hundreds of years,' said Bina. 'They were quite happy without the dam, weren't they?'

'I suppose they were. But the dam isn't just for them—it's for the millions who live further downstream, across the plains.'

'And it doesn't matter what happens to this place?'

'The local people will be given new homes, somewhere else.' Miss Ramola found herself on the defensive and decided to change the subject. 'Everyone must be hungry. It's time we had our lunch.'

Bina kept quiet. She didn't think the local people would want to go away. And it was a good thing, she mused, that there was only a small stream and not a big river running past her village. To be uprooted like this—a town and hundreds of villages—and put down somewhere on the hot, dusty plains—

seemed to her unbearable.

'Well, I'm glad I don't live in Tehri,' she said.

She did not know it, but all the animals and most of the birds had already left the area. The leopard had been among them.

They walked through the colourful, crowded bazaar, where fruit sellers did business beside silversmiths, and pavement vendors sold everything from umbrellas to glass bangles. Sparrows attacked sacks of grain, monkeys made off with bananas, and stray cows and dogs rummaged in refuse bins, but nobody took any notice. Music blared from radios. Buses blew their horns. Sonu bought a whistle to add to the general din, but Miss Ramola told him to put it away. Bina had kept ten rupees aside, and now she used it to buy a cotton head scarf for her mother.

As they were about to enter a small restaurant for a meal, they were joined by Prakash and his companions; but of Mr Mani there was still no sign.

'He must have met one of his relatives,' said Prakash. 'He has relatives everywhere.'

After a simple meal of rice and lentils, they walked the length of the bazaar without seeing Mr Mani. At last, when they were about to give up the search, they saw him emerge from a bylane, a large sack slung over his shoulder.

'Sir, where have you been?' asked Prakash. 'We have been looking for you everywhere.'

On Mr Mani's face was a look of triumph.

'Help me with this bag,' he said breathlessly.

'You've bought more potatoes, sir,' said Prakash.

'Not potatoes, boy. Dahlia bulbs!'

7

It was dark by the time they were all back in Nauti. Mr Mani had refused to be separated from his sack of dahlia bulbs, and had been forced to sit in the back of the truck with Prakash and most of the boys.

Bina did not feel so ill on the return journey. Going uphill was definitely better than going downhill! But by the time the bus reached Nauti it was too late for most of the children to walk back to the more distant villages. The boys were put up in different homes, while the girls were given beds in the school verandah.

The night was warm and still. Large moths fluttered around the single bulb that lit the verandah. Counting moths, Sonu soon fell asleep. But Bina stayed awake for some time, listening to the sounds of the night. A nightjar went *tonk-tonk* in the bushes, and somewhere in the forest an owl hooted softly. The sharp call of a barking deer travelled up the valley, from the direction of the stream. Jackals kept howling. It seemed that there were more of them than ever before.

Bina was not the only one to hear the barking deer. The leopard, stretched full length on a rocky ledge, heard it too. The leopard raised its head and then got up slowly. The deer was its natural prey. But there weren't many left, and that was why the leopard, robbed of its forest by the dam, had taken to attacking dogs and cattle near the villages.

As the cry of the barking deer sounded nearer, the leopard left its lookout point and moved swiftly through the shadows towards the stream.

In early June the hills were dry and dusty, and forest fires broke out, destroying shrubs and trees, killing birds and small animals. The resin in the pines made these trees burn more fiercely, and the wind would take sparks from the trees and carry them into the dry grass and leaves, so that new fires would spring up before the old ones had died out. Fortunately, Bina's village was not in the pine belt; the fires did not reach it. But Nauti was surrounded by a fire that raged for three days, and the children had to stay away from school.

And then, towards the end of June, the monsoon rains arrived and there was an end to forest fires. The monsoon lasts three months and the lower Himalayas would be drenched in rain, mist and cloud for the next three months.

The first rain arrived while Bina, Prakash and Sonu were returning home from school. Those first few drops on the dusty path made them cry out with excitement. Then the rain grew heavier and a wonderful aroma rose from the earth.

'The best smell in the world!' exclaimed Bina.

Everything suddenly came to life. The grass, the crops, the trees, the birds. Even the leaves of the trees glistened and looked new.

That first wet weekend, Bina and Sonu helped their mother plant beans, maize and cucumbers. Sometimes, when the rain was very heavy, they had to run indoors. Otherwise they worked in the rain, the soft mud clinging to their bare legs.

Prakash now owned a black dog with one ear up and one ear down. The dog ran around getting in everyone's way, barking at cows, goats, hens and humans, without frightening any of them. Prakash said it was a very clever dog, but no one else seemed to think so. Prakash also said it would protect the village from the leopard, but others said the dog would be the first to be taken—he'd run straight into the jaws of Mr Spots!

In Nauti, Tania Ramola was trying to find a dry spot in the quarters she'd been given. It was an old building and the roof was leaking in several places. Mugs and buckets were scattered about the floor in order to catch the drip.

Mr Mani had dug up all his potatoes and presented them to the friends and neighbours who had given him lunches and dinners. He was having the time of his life, planting dahlia bulbs all over his garden.

'I'll have a field of many-coloured dahlias!' he announced. 'Just wait till the end of August!'

'Watch out for those porcupines,' warned his sister. 'They eat dahlia bulbs too!'

Mr Mani made an inspection tour of his moat, no longer in flood, and found everything in good order. Prakash had done his job well.

Now, when the children crossed the stream, they found that the water level had risen by about a foot. Small cascades had turned into waterfalls. Ferns had sprung up on the banks. Frogs chanted.

Prakash and his dog dashed across the stream. Bina and Sonu followed more cautiously. The current was much stronger now and the water was almost up to their knees. Once they had crossed the stream, they hurried along the path, anxious not to be caught in a sudden downpour.

By the time they reached school, each of them had two or three leeches clinging to their legs. They had to use salt to remove them. The leeches were the most troublesome part of the rainy season. Even the leopard did not like them. It could not lie in the long grass without getting leeches on its paws and face.

One day, when Bina, Prakash and Sonu were about to cross the stream they heard a low rumble, which grew louder every second. Looking up at the opposite hill, they saw several trees shudder, tilt outwards and begin to fall. Earth and rocks bulged out from the mountain, then came crashing down into the ravine.

'Landslide!' shouted Sonu.

'It's carried away the path,' said Bina. 'Don't go any further.'

There was a tremendous roar as more rocks, trees and bushes fell away and crashed down the hillside.

Prakash's dog, who had gone ahead, came running back, tail between his legs.

They remained rooted to the spot until the rocks had stopped falling and the dust had settled. Birds circled the area, calling wildly. A frightened barking deer ran past them.

'We can't go to school now,' said Prakash. 'There's no way around.'

They turned and trudged home through the gathering mist.

In Koli, Prakash's parents had heard the roar of the landslide. They were setting out in search of the children when they saw them emerge from the mist, waving cheerfully.

9

They had to miss school for another three days, and Bina was afraid they might not be able to take their final exams. Although Prakash was not really troubled at the thought of missing exams, he did not like feeling helpless just because their path had been swept away. So he explored the hillside until he found a goat track going around the mountain. It joined up with another path near Nauti. This made their walk longer by a mile, but

Bina did not mind. It was much cooler now that the rains were in full swing.

The only trouble with the new route was that it passed close to the leopard's lair. The animal had made this area its own since being forced to leave the dam area.

One day Prakash's dog ran ahead of them, barking furiously. Then he ran back, whimpering.

'He's always running away from something,' observed Sonu. But a minute later he understood the reason for the dog's fear.

They rounded a bend and Sonu saw the leopard standing in their way. They were struck dumb—too terrified to run. It was a strong, sinewy creature. A low growl rose from its throat. It seemed ready to spring.

They stood perfectly still, afraid to move or say a word. And the leopard must have been equally surprised. It stared at them for a few seconds, then bounded across the path and into the oak forest.

Sonu was shaking. Bina could hear her heart hammering. Prakash could only stammer: 'Did you see the way he sprang? Wasn't he beautiful?'

He forgot to look at his watch for the rest of the day.

A few days later Sonu stopped and pointed to a large outcrop of rock on the next hill.

The leopard stood far above them, outlined against the sky. It looked strong, majestic. Standing beside it were two young cubs.

'Look at those little ones!' exclaimed Sonu.

'So it's a female, not a male,' said Prakash.

'That's why she was killing so often,' said Bina. 'She had to feed her cubs too.'

They remained still for several minutes, gazing up at the leopard and her cubs. The leopard family took no notice of them.

'She knows we are here,' said Prakash, 'but she doesn't care. She knows we won't harm them.'

'We are cubs too!' said Sonu.

'Yes,' said Bina. 'And there's still plenty of space for all of us. Even when the dam is ready there will still be room for leopards and humans.'

10

The school exams were over. The rains were nearly over too. The landslide had been cleared, and Bina, Prakash and Sonu were once again crossing the stream.

There was a chill in the air, for it was the end of September.

Prakash had learnt to play the flute quite well, and he played on the way to school and then again on the way home. As a result he did not look at his watch so often.

One morning they found a small crowd in front of Mr Mani's house.

'What could have happened?' wondered Bina. 'I hope he hasn't got lost again.'

'Maybe he's sick,' said Sonu.

'Maybe it's the porcupines,' said Prakash.

But it was none of these things.

Mr Mani's first dahlia was in bloom, and half the village had turned out to look at it! It was a huge red double dahlia, so heavy that it had to be supported with sticks. No one had ever seen such a magnificent flower!

Mr Mani was a happy man. And his mood only improved over the coming week, as more and more dahlias flowered—crimson, yellow, purple, mauve, white—button dahlias, pompom dahlias, spotted dahlias, striped dahlias…Mr Mani had them all! A dahlia even turned up on Tania Romola's desk—he got on quite well with her now—and another brightened up the headmaster's study.

A week later, on their way home—it was almost the last day of the school term—Bina, Prakash and Sonu talked about what they might do when they grew up.

'I think I'll become a teacher,' said Bina. 'I'll teach children about animals and birds, and trees and flowers.'

'Better than maths!' said Prakash.

'I'll be a pilot,' said Sonu. 'I want to fly a plane like Miss Ramola's brother.'

'And what about you, Prakash?' asked Bina.

Prakash just smiled and said, 'Maybe I'll be a flute player,' and he put the flute to his lips and played a sweet melody.

'Well, the world needs flute players too,' said Bina, as they fell into step beside him.

The leopard had been stalking a barking deer. She paused when she heard the flute and the voices of the children. Her own young ones were growing quickly, but the girl and the two boys did not look much older.

They had started singing their favourite song again:

Five more miles to go!
We climb through rain and snow.
A river to cross…
A mountain to pass…
Now we've four more miles to go!

The leopard waited until they had passed, before returning to the trail of the barking deer.

CRICKET FOR THE CROCODILE

Ranji was up at dawn.

It was Sunday, a school holiday. Although he was supposed to be preparing for his exams, only a fortnight away, he couldn't resist one or two more games before getting down to history and algebra and other unexciting things.

'I'm going to be a Test cricketer when I grow up,' he told his mother. 'Of what use will maths be to me?'

'You never know,' said his mother, who happened to be more of a cricket fan than his father. 'You might need maths to work out your batting average. And as for history, wouldn't you like to be a part of history? Famous cricketers make history!'

'Making history is all right,' said Ranji. 'As long as I don't have to remember the date on which I make it!'

♦

Ranji met his friends and teammates in the park. The grass was still wet with dew, the sun only just rising behind the distant hills. The park was full of flower beds, and swings and slides for smaller children. The boys would have to play on the riverbank against their rivals, the village boys. Ranji did not have a full team that morning, but he was looking for a 'friendly' match. The really important game would be held the following Sunday.

The village team was quite good because the boys lived near each other and practised a lot together, whereas Ranji's team was drawn from all parts of the town. There was the baker's boy, Nathu; the tailor's son, Sunder; the postmaster's son, Prem; and the bank manager's son, Anil. These were some of the better players. Sometimes their fathers also turned up for a game. The fathers weren't very good, but you couldn't tell them that. After all, they helped to provide bats and balls and pocket money.

A regular spectator at these matches was Nakoo, the crocodile, who lived in the river. Nakoo means Nosey, but the village boys were very respectful and called him Nakoo-ji, Nakoo sir. He had a long snout, rows of ugly-looking teeth (some of them badly in need of fillings), and a powerful, scaly tail.

He was nearly fifteen feet long, but you did not see much of him; he swam low in the water and glided smoothly through the tall grasses near the river. Sometimes he came out on the riverbank to bask in the sun. He did not care for people, especially cricketers. He disliked the noise they made, frightening away the waterbirds and other creatures required for an interesting menu, and it was also alarming to have cricket balls plopping around in the shallows where he liked to rest.

Once Nakoo crept quite close to the bank manager, who was resting against one of the trees near the riverbank. The bank manager was a portly gentleman, and Nakoo seemed to think he would make a good meal. Just then a party of villagers had come along, beating drums for a marriage party. Nakoo retired to the muddy waters of the river. He was a little tired of swallowing frogs, eels and herons. That juicy bank manager would make a nice change—he'd grab him one day!

◆

The village boys were a little bigger than Ranji and his friends, but they did not bring their fathers along. The game made very little sense to the older villagers. And when balls came flying across fields to land in milk pails or cooking pots, they were as annoyed as the crocodile.

Today, the men were busy in the fields, and Nakoo was wallowing in the mud behind a screen of reeds and water lilies. How beautiful and innocent those lilies looked! Only sharp eyes would have noticed Nakoo's long snout thrusting above the broad, flat leaves of the lilies. His eyes were slits. He was watching.

Ranji struck the ball hard and high. Splash! It fell into the river about thirty feet from where Nakoo lay. Village boys and town boys dashed into the shallow water to look for the ball. Too many of them! Crowds made Nakoo nervous. He slid away, crossed the river to the opposite bank, and sulked.

As it was a warm day, nobody seemed to want to get out of the water. Several boys threw off their clothes, deciding that it was a better day for swimming than for cricket. Nakoo's mouth watered as he watched those bare limbs splashing about.

'We're supposed to be practising,' said Ranji, who took his cricket seriously. 'We won't win next week.'

'Oh, we'll win easily,' said Anil, joining him on the riverbank. 'My father says he's going to play.'

'The last time he played, we lost,' said Ranji. 'He made two runs and forgot to field.'

'He was out of form,' said Anil, ever loyal to his father,

the bank manager.

Sheroo, the captain of the village team, joined them. 'My cousin from Delhi is going to play for us. He made a hundred in one of the matches there.'

'He won't make a hundred on this wicket,' said Ranji. 'It's slow at one end and fast at the other.'

'Can I bring my father?' asked Nathu, the baker's son.

'Can he play?'

'Not too well, but he'll bring along a basket of biscuits, buns and pakoras.'

'Then he can play,' said Ranji, always quick to make up his mind. No wonder he was the team's captain! 'If there are too many of us, we'll make him twelfth man.'

The ball could not be found, and as they did not want to risk their spare ball, the practice session was declared over.

'My grandfather's promised me a new ball,' said little Mani, from the village team, who bowled tricky leg breaks which bounced off to the side.

'Does he want to play, too?' asked Ranji.

'No, of course not. He's nearly eighty.'

'That's settled, then,' said Ranji. 'We'll all meet here at nine o'clock next Sunday. Fifty overs a side.'

They broke up, Sheroo and his team wandering back to the village, while Ranji and his friends got onto their bicycles (two or three to a bicycle, since not everyone had one), and cycled back to town.

Nakoo, left in peace at last, returned to his favourite side of the river and crawled some way up the riverbank, as if to inspect the wicket. It had been worn smooth by the players, and looked like a good place to relax. Nakoo moved across it. He felt pleasantly drowsy in the warm sun, so he closed his eyes for a little nap. It was good to be out of the water for a while.

◆

The following Sunday morning, a cycle bell tinkled at the gate. It was Nathu, waiting for Ranji to join him. Ranji hurried out of the house, carrying his bat and a thermos of lime juice thoughtfully provided by his mother.

'Have you got the stumps?' he asked.

'Sunder has them.'

'And the ball?'

'Yes. And Anil's father is bringing one too, provided he opens the batting!'

Nathu rode, while Ranji sat on the cross bar with bat and thermos. Anil was waiting for them outside his house.

'My father's gone ahead on his scooter. He's picking up Nathu's father. I'll follow with Prem and Sunder.'

Most of the boys got to the riverbank before the bank manager and the baker. They left their bicycles under a shady banyan tree and ran down the gentle slope to the river. And then, one by one, they stopped, astonished by what they saw.

They gaped in awe at their cricket pitch. Across it, basking in the soft warm sunshine, was Nakoo the crocodile.

'Where did it come from?' asked Ranji.

'Usually he stays in the river,' said Sheroo, who had joined them. 'But all this week he's been coming out to lie on our wicket. I don't think he wants us to play.'

'We'll have to get him off,' said Ranji.

'You'd better keep out of reach of his tail and jaws!'

'We'll wait until he goes away,' said Prem.

But Nakoo showed no signs of wanting to leave. He rather liked the smooth, flat stretch of ground which he had discovered.

And here were all the boys again, doing their best to disturb him.

After some time the boys began throwing pebbles at Nakoo. These had no effect, simply bouncing off the crocodile's tough hide. They tried mud balls and an orange. Nakoo twitched his tail and opened one eye, but refused to move on.

Then Prem took a ball, and bowled a fast one at the crocodile. It bounced just short of Nakoo and caught him on the snout. Startled and stung, he wriggled off the pitch and moved rapidly down the riverbank and into the water. There was a mighty splash as he dived for cover.

'Well bowled, Prem!' said Ranji. 'That was a good ball.'

'Nakoo-ji will be in a bad mood after that,' warned Sheroo. 'Don't get too close to the river.'

The bank manager and the baker were the last to arrive. The scooter had given them some trouble. No one mentioned the crocodile, just in case the adults decided to call the match off.

After inspecting the wicket, which Nakoo had left in fair condition, Sheroo and Ranji tossed a coin. Ranji called 'Heads!' but it came up tails. Sheroo chose to bat first.

◆

The tall Delhi player came out to open the innings with little Mani.

Mani was a steady bat, who could stay at the wicket for a long time; but in a one-day match, quick scoring was needed. This the Delhi player provided. He struck a four, then took a single off the last ball of the over.

In the third over, Mani tried to hit out and was bowled for a duck. So the village team's score was 13 for 1.

'Well done,' said Ranji to fast bowler Prem. 'But we'll have to get that tall fellow out soon. He seems quite good.'

The tall fellow showed no sign of getting out. He hit two more boundaries and then swung one hard and high towards the river.

Nakoo, who had been sulking in the shallows, saw the ball coming towards him. He opened his jaws wide, and with a satisfying 'clunk!' the ball lodged between his back teeth.

Nakoo got his teeth deep into the cricket ball and chewed. Revenge was sweet. And the ball tasted good, too. The combination of leather and cork was just right. Nakoo decided that he would snap up any other balls that came his way.

'Harmless old reptile,' said the bank manager. He produced a new ball and insisted that he bowl with it.

It proved to be the most expensive over of the match. The bank manager's bowling was quite harmless and the Delhi player kept hitting the ball into the fields for fours and sixes. The score soon mounted to 40 for 1. The bank manager modestly took himself off.

By the time the tenth over had been bowled, the score had mounted to 70. Then Ranji, bowling slow spin, lost his grip on the ball and sent the batsman a full toss. Having played the good balls perfectly, the Delhi player couldn't resist taking a mighty swipe at the bad ball. He mistimed his shot and was astonished to see the ball fall into the hands of a fielder near the boundary. 70 for 2. The game was far from being lost for Ranji's team.

A couple of wickets fell cheaply, and then Sheroo came in and started playing rather well. His drives were straight and clean. The ball cut down the buttercups and hummed over the grass. A big hit landed in a poultry yard. Feathers flew and so did curses. Nakoo raised his head to see what all the noise was about. No further cricket balls came his way, and he gazed balefully at a heron who was staying just out of his reach.

The score mounted steadily. The fielding grew slack, as it often does when batsmen gain the upper hand. A catch was dropped. And Nathu's father, keeping wicket, missed a stumping chance.

'No more grown-ups in our team,' grumbled Nathu.

The baker made amends by taking a good catch behind the wicket. The score was 115 for 5, with about half the overs remaining.

Sheroo kept his end up, but the remaining batsmen struggled for runs and the end came with about 5 overs still to go. A modest total of 145.

'Should be easy,' said Ranji.

'No problem,' said Prem.

'Lunch first,' said the bank manager, and they took a half-hour break.

The village boys went to their homes for rest and refreshment, while Ranji and his team spread themselves out under the banyan tree.

Nathu's father had brought patties and pakoras; the bank manager brought a basket of oranges and bananas; Prem had brought a jackfruit curry; Ranji had brought a halwa made from carrots, milk and sugar; Sunder had brought a large container full of pulao rice cooked with peas and fried onions; and the others had brought various curries, pickles, and sauces. Everything was shared, and with the picnic in full swing no one noticed that Nakoo the crocodile had left the water. Using some tall reeds as cover, he had crept halfway up the riverbank. Those delicious food smells had reached him too, and he was unwilling to be left out of the picnic. Perhaps the boys would leave something for him. If not...

'Time to start,' announced the bank manager, getting up. 'I'll open the batting. We need a good start if we are going to win!'

◆

The bank manager strode out to the wicket in the company of young Nathu. Sheroo opened the bowling for the village team.

The bank manager took a run off the first ball. He puffed himself up and waved his bat in the air as though the match had already been won. Nathu played out the rest of the over without taking any chances.

The tall Delhi player took up the bowling from the other end. The bank manager tapped his bat impatiently, then raised it above his shoulders, ready to hit out. The bowler took a long, fast run up to the bowling crease. He gave a little leap, his arm swung over, and the ball came at the bank manager in a swift, curving flight.

The bank manager still had his bat raised when the ball flew past him and uprooted his middle stump.

A shout of joy went up from the fielders. The bank manager was on his way back to the shade of the banyan tree.

'A fly got in my eye,' he muttered. 'I wasn't ready. Flies everywhere!' And he swatted angrily at flies that no one else could see.

The villagers, hearing that someone as important as a bank manager was in their midst, decided that it would be wrong for him to sit on the ground like everyone else. So they brought him a cot from the village. It was one of those light wooden beds, taped with strands of thin rope. The bank manager lowered himself into it rather gingerly. It creaked but took his weight.

The score was 1 for 1.

Anil took his father's place at the wicket and scored 10

runs in two overs. The bank manager pretended not to notice but he was really quite pleased. 'Takes after me,' he said, and made himself comfortable on the cot.

Nathu kept his end up while Anil scored the runs. Then Anil was out, skying a catch to midwicket.

25 for 2 in six overs. It could have been worse.

'Well played!' called the bank manager to his son, and then lost interest in the proceedings. He was soon fast asleep on the cot. The flies did not seem to bother him any more.

Nathu kept going, and there were a couple of good partnerships for the fourth and fifth wickets. When the Delhi player finished his share of overs, the batsmen became more free in their stroke play. Then little Mani got a ball to spin sharply, and Nathu was caught by the wicketkeeper.

It was 75 for 4 when Ranji came in to bat.

Before he could score a run, his partner at the other end was bowled. And then Nathu's father strode up to the wicket, determined to do better than the bank manager. In this, he succeeded by 1 run.

The baker scored 2, and then in trying to run another 2 when there was only one to be had, found himself stranded halfway up the wicket. The wicketkeeper knocked his stumps down.

The boys were too polite to say anything. And as for the bank manager he was now fast asleep under the banyan tree.

So intent was everyone on watching the cricket that no one noticed that Nakoo, the crocodile, had crept further up the riverbank to slide beneath the cot on which the bank manager was sleeping.

There was just room enough for Nakoo to get between the legs of the cot. He thought it was a good place to lie concealed, and he seemed not to notice the large man sleeping peacefully just above him.

Soon the bank manager was snoring gently, and it was not long before Nakoo dozed off, too. Only, instead of snoring, Nakoo appeared to be whistling through his crooked teeth.

◆

75 for 5 and it looked as though Ranji's team would soon be crashing to defeat.

Sunder joined Ranji and, to everyone's delight, played two lovely drives to the boundary. Then Ranji got into his stride and cut and drove the ball for successive fours. The score began to mount steadily. 112 for 5. Once again there were visions of victory.

After Sunder was out, stumped, Ranji was joined by Prem, a big hitter. Runs came quickly. The score reached 140. Only 6 runs were needed for victory.

Ranji decided to do it in style. Receiving a half-volley, he drove the ball hard and high towards the banyan tree.

Thump! It struck Nakoo on the jaw and loosened one of his teeth.

It was the second time that day he'd been caught napping. He'd had enough of it.

Nakoo lunged forward, tail thrashing and jaws snapping. The cot, with the manager still on it, rose with him. Crocodile and cot were now jammed together, and when Nakoo rushed forward, he took the cot with him.

The bank manager, dreaming that he was at sea in a rowing boat, woke up to find the cot pitching violently from side to side.

'Help!' he shouted. 'Help!'

The boys scattered in all directions, for the crocodile was now advancing down the wicket, knocking over stumps and digging up the pitch. He found an abandoned sun hat and swallowed it. A wicketkeeper's glove went the same way. A batsman's pad was caught up on his tail.

All this time the bank manager hung on to the cot for safety, but would he be able to get out of reach of Nakoo's jaw and tail? He decided to hang on to the cot until it was dislodged.

'Come on, boys, help!' he shouted. 'Get me off!'

But the cot remained firmly attached to the crocodile, and so did the bank manager.

The problem was solved when Nakoo made for the river and plunged into its familiar waters. Then the bank manager tumbled into the water and scrambled up the bank, while Nakoo made for the opposite shore.

The bank manager's ordeal was over, and so was the cricket match.

'Did you see how I dealt with that crocodile?' he said, still dripping, but in better humour now that he was safe again. 'By the way, who won the match?'

'We don't know,' said Ranji, as they trudged back to their bicycles. 'That would have been a 6 if you hadn't been in the way.'

Sheroo, who had accompanied them as far as the main road, offered a return match the following week.

'I'm busy next week,' said the baker.

'I have another game,' said the bank manager.

'What game is that, sir?' asked Ranji.

'Chess,' said the bank manager.

Ranji and his friends began making plans for the next match. 'You won't win without us,' said the bank manager.

'Not a chance,' said the baker.

But Ranji's team did, in fact, win the next match.

Nakoo the crocodile did not trouble them because the cot was still attached to his back, and it took him several weeks to get it off.

A number of people came to the riverbank to look at the crocodile who carried his own bed around.

Some even stayed to watch the cricket.

RANJI'S WONDERFUL BAT

'How's that!' shouted the wicketkeeper, holding the ball up in his gloves.

'How's that!' echoed the slip fielders.

'How?' growled the fast bowler, glaring at the umpire.

'Out!' said the umpire.

And Suraj, the captain of the school team, was walking slowly back to the pavilion—which was really a toolshed at the end of the field.

The score stood at 53 runs for 4 wickets. Another 60 runs had to be made for victory, and only one good batsman remained. All the rest were bowlers who couldn't be expected to make many runs.

It was Ranji's turn to bat.

He was the youngest member of the team, only eleven, but sturdy and full of pluck. As he walked briskly to the wicket, his unruly black hair was blown about by a cool breeze that came down from the hills.

Ranji had a good eye and strong wrists, and had made lots of runs in some of the minor matches. But in the last two inter-school games, his scores had been poor, the highest being 12 runs. Today he was determined to make enough runs to take his side to victory.

Ranji took his guard and prepared to face the bowler. The fielders moved closer, in anticipation of another catch. The tall fast bowler scowled and began his long run. His arm whirled over, and the hard, shiny red ball came hurtling towards Ranji.

Ranji was going to lunge forward and play the ball back to the bowler, but at the last moment he changed his mind and stepped back, intending to push the ball through the ring of fielders on his right or offside.

'How's that!' screamed the bowler hopping about like a kangaroo.

'How?' shouted the wicketkeeper.

The umpire slowly raised a finger.

'Out,' he said.

'Never mind,' said Suraj, patting Ranji on the back. 'You'll do better next time. You're out of form just now, that's all.'

'You'll have to make more runs in the next game,' he told Ranji, 'or you'll lose your place in the side!'

Avoiding the other players, Ranji slowly walked homewards, his head down, his hands in his pockets. He was very upset. He had been trying so hard and practising so regularly, but when an important game came along he failed to make a big score. It seemed that there was nothing he could do about it. But he loved playing cricket, and he couldn't bear the thought of being out of the school team.

On his way home he had to pass the clock tower, where he often stopped at Mr Kumar's Sports Shop, to chat with the owner or look at all the things on the shelves: footballs, cricket balls, badminton rackets, hockey sticks, balls of various shapes and sizes—it was a wonderland where Ranji liked to linger every day.

But this was one day when he didn't feel like stopping. He looked the other way and was about to cross the road when Mr Kumar's voice stopped him.

'Hello, Ranji! Off in a hurry today? And why are you looking so sad?'

So Ranji had to stop and say namaste. He couldn't ignore Mr Kumar, who had always been so kind and helpful, often giving him advice on how to bowl in different styles. Mr Kumar had been a state-level player once, and had scored a century in a match against Tanzania. Now he liked encouraging young players and he thought Ranji would make a good cricketer.

'What's the trouble?' he asked as Ranji stepped into the shop. Because Mr Kumar was so friendly, the sports merchandise also seemed friendly. The bats and balls and shuttlecocks all seemed to want to be helpful.

'We lost the match,' said Ranji.

'Never mind,' said Mr Kumar. 'Where would we be without losers? There wouldn't be any games without them—no cricket or football or hockey or tennis! No carom or marbles. No sports shop for me! Anyway, how many runs did you make?'

'None, I made a big, round egg.'

Mr Kumar rested his hand on Ranji's shoulder. 'Never mind. All good players have a bad day now and then.'

'But I haven't made a good score in my last three matches,' said Ranji. 'I'll be dropped from the team if I don't do something in the next game.'

'Well, we can't have that happening,' mused Mr Kumar.

'Something will have to be done about it.'

'I'm just unlucky,' said Ranji.

'Maybe, maybe... But in that case, it's time your luck changed.'

'It's too late now,' said Ranji.

'Nonsense. It's never too late. Now, you just come with me to the back of the shop and I'll see if I can do something about your luck.'

Puzzled, Ranji followed Mr Kumar through the curtained partition at the back of the shop. He found himself in a badly-lit room stacked to the ceiling with all kinds of old and second-hand sporting goods—torn football bladders, broken bats, rackets without strings, broken darts, and tattered badminton nets. Mr Kumar began examining a number of old cricket bats, and after a few minutes he said, 'Ah!' Picking up one of the bats, he held it out to Ranji.

'This is it!' he said. 'This is the luckiest of all my old bats. This is the bat I made a century with!' He gave it a twirl and started hitting an imaginary ball to all corners of the room.

'Of course it's an old bat, but it hasn't lost any of its magic,' said Mr Kumar, pausing in his stroke-making to recover his breath. He held it out to Ranji. 'Here, take it!' I'll lend it to you for the rest of the cricket season. You won't fail with this with you.'

Ranji took the bat and looked at it with awe and delight.

'Is it really the bat you made a century with?' he asked.

'It is,' said Mr Kumar. 'And it may get you a hundred runs too!'

Ranji spent a nervous week waiting for Saturday's match. His school team would be playing against a strong side from another town. There was a lot of classwork that week, so Ranji did not get much time to practise with the other boys. As he had no brothers or sisters he asked Koki, the girl next door, to bowl to him in the garden. Koki bowled quite well, but Ranji liked to hit the ball hard—'just to get used to the bat,' he told her—and she soon got tired of chasing the ball all over the garden.

At last Saturday arrived, bright and sunny and just right for cricket.

Suraj won the toss for the school and chose batting first.

The opening batsmen put on 30 runs without being separated. The visiting fast bowlers couldn't do much. Then the spin bowlers came on, and immediately there was a change in the game. Two wickets fell in one over, and the score was 33 for 2. Suraj made a few quick runs, then he too was out to one of the spinners, caught behind the wicket. The next batsman was clean bowled—46 for 4—and it was Ranji's turn to bat.

He walked slowly to the wicket. The fielders crowded around him. He took guard and prepared for the first ball.

The bowler took a short run and then the ball was twirling towards Ranji, looking as though it would spin away from his bat as he leaned forward into his stroke.

And then a thrill ran through Ranji's arm as he felt the ball meet the springy willow of the bat.

Crack!

The ball, hit firmly with the middle of Ranji's bat, streaked past the helpless bowler and sped towards the boundary. Four runs!

The bowler was annoyed, with the result that his next ball was a loose full toss. Ranji swung it to the onside boundary for another four.

And that was only the beginning. Now, Ranji began to

play all the strokes he knew: late cuts and square cuts, straight drives, on drives and off drives. The rival captain tried all his bowlers, fast and spin, but none of them could remove Ranji. Instead, he sent the fielders scampering to all corners of the field.

By the lunch break he had scored 40 runs. And twenty minutes after lunch, when Suraj closed the innings, Ranji was not out with 58.

The rival team was bowled out for a poor score, and Ranji's school won the match.

On his way home, Ranji stopped at Mr Kumar's shop to give him the good news.

'We won!' he said. 'And I made 58—my highest score so far. It really is a lucky bat!'

'I told you so,' said Mr Kumar, giving Ranji a warm handshake. 'There will be bigger scores yet.'

Ranji went home in high spirits. He was so pleased that he stopped at the Jumma Sweet Shop and bought two laddus for Koki. She was crazy about laddus.

Mr Kumar was right. It was only the beginning of Ranji's success with the bat. In the next game he scored 40, and was out when he grew careless and allowed himself to be stumped by the wicketkeeper. The game that followed was a two-day match, and Ranji, who was now batting at Number 3, made 45 runs. He hit a number of boundaries before being caught. In the second innings, when the school team needed only 6 runs for victory, Ranji was batting at 25 when the winning runs were hit.

Everyone was pleased with him—his coach, his captain, Suraj, and Mr Kumar—but only one knew about the lucky bat. That was a secret between Ranji and Mr Kumar.

One evening, during an informal game on the maidan,

Ranji's friend Bhim slipped while running after the ball, and cut his hand on a sharp stone. Ranji took him to a doctor near the clock tower, where the wound was washed and bandaged. As it was getting late, he decided to go straight home. Usually he walked, but that evening he caught a bus near the clock tower.

When he got home, his mother brought him a cup of tea, and while he was drinking it, Koki walked in, and the first thing she said was, 'Ranji, where's your bat?'

'Oh, I must have left it at the maidan when Bhim got hurt,' said Ranji, starting up and spilling his tea. 'I'd better go and get it now, or it will disappear.'

'You can fetch it tomorrow,' said his mother. 'It's getting dark.'

'I'll take a torch,' said Ranji.

He was worried about the bat.

Without it, his luck might desert him.

He hadn't the patience to wait for a bus, and ran all the way to the maidan.

The maidan was deserted, and there was no sign of the bat. And then Ranji remembered that he'd had it with him on the bus, after saying goodbye to Bhim at the clock tower. He must have left it on the bus!

Well, he'd never find it now. The bat was lost forever. And on Saturday Ranji's school would be playing their last and most important match of the cricket season against a public school team from Delhi.

Next day he was at Mr Kumar's shop, looking very sorry for himself.

'What's the matter?' asked Mr Kumar.

'I've lost the bat,' said Ranji. 'Your lucky bat. The one I made all my runs with! I left it in the bus. And the day after tomorrow we are playing the Delhi school, and I'll be out for a duck, and we'll lose our chance of being the champion school.'

Mr Kumar looked a little anxious at first; then he smiled and said, 'You can still make all the runs you want.'

'But I don't have the bat any more,' said Ranji.

'Any bat will do,' said Mr Kumar.

'What do you mean?'

'I mean it's the batsman and not the bat that matters. Shall I tell you something? That old bat I gave you was no different from any other bat I've used. True, I made a lot of runs with it, but I made runs with other bats too. A bat has magic only when the batsman has magic! What you needed was confidence, not a bat. And by believing in the bat, you got your confidence back!'

'What's confidence?' asked Ranji. It was a new word for him.

'Confidence,' said Mr Kumar slowly, 'confidence is knowing you are good.'

'And I can be good without the bat?'

'Of course. You have always been good. You are good now. You will be good the day after tomorrow. Remember that. If you remember it, you'll make the runs.'

On Saturday, Ranji walked to the wicket with a bat borrowed from Bhim.

The school team had lost its first wicket with only 2 runs on the board. Ranji went in at this stage. The Delhi school's opening bowler was sending down some really fast ones. Ranji faced up to him.

The first ball was very fast but it wasn't on a good length. Quick on his feet, Ranji stepped back and pulled it hard to the onside boundary. The ball soared over the heads of the fielders and landed with a crash in a crate full of cold drink bottles.

A six! Everyone stood up and cheered.

And it was only the beginning of Ranji's wonderful innings.

The match ended in a draw, but Ranji's 75 was the talk of the school.

On his way home he bought a dozen laddus. Six for Koki and six for Mr Kumar.

THE LONG DAY

Suraj was awakened by the sound of his mother busying herself in the kitchen. He lay in bed, looking through the open window at the sky getting lighter and the dawn pushing its way into the room. He knew there was something important about this new day, but for some time he couldn't remember what it was. Then, as the room cleared, his mind cleared. His school report would be arriving in the post.

Suraj knew he had failed. The class teacher had told him so. But his mother would only know of it when she read the report, and Suraj did not want to be in the house when she received it. He was sure it would be arriving today. So he had told his mother that he would be having his midday meal with his friend Somi—Somi, who wasn't even in town at the moment—and would be home only for the evening meal. By that time, he hoped, his mother would have recovered from the shock. He was glad his father was away on tour.

He slipped out of bed and went to the kitchen. His mother was surprised to see him up so early.

'I'm going for a walk, Ma,' he said, 'and then I'll go on to Somi's house.'

'Well, have your bath first and put something in your stomach.'

Suraj went to the tap in the courtyard and took a quick bath. He put on a clean shirt and shorts. Carelessly, he brushed his thick, curly hair, knowing he couldn't bring much order to its wildness. Then he gulped down a glass of milk and hurried out of the house. The postman wouldn't arrive for a couple of hours, but Suraj felt that the earlier his start the better. His mother was surprised and pleased to see him up and about so early.

Suraj was out on the maidaan and still the sun had not risen. The maidaan was an open area of grass, about a hundred square metres, and from the middle of it could be seen the mountains, range upon range of them, stepping into the sky. A game of football was in progress, and one of the players called out to Suraj to join them. Suraj said he wouldn't play for more than ten minutes, because he had some business to attend to; he kicked off his chappals and ran barefoot after the ball. Everyone was playing barefoot. It was an informal game, and the players were of all ages and sizes, from bearded Sikhs to small boys of six or seven. Suraj ran all over the place without actually getting in touch with the ball—he wasn't much good at football—and finally got into a scramble before the goal, fell and scratched his knee. He retired from the game even sooner than he had intended.

The scratch wasn't bad but there was some blood on his knee. He wiped it clean with his handkerchief and limped off the maidaan. He went in the direction of the railway station, but not through the bazaar. He went by way of the canal, which came from the foot of the nearest mountain, flowed through the town and down to the river. Beside the canal were the washerwomen, scrubbing and beating out clothes on the stone banks.

The canal was only a metre wide but, due to recent rain, the current was swift and noisy. Suraj stood on the bank, watching the rush of water. There was an inlet at one place, and here some children were bathing, and some were rushing up and down the bank, wearing nothing at all, shouting to each other in high spirits. Suraj felt like taking a dip too, but he did not know any of the children here; most of them were from very poor families. Hands in pockets, he walked along the canal banks.

The sun had risen and was pouring through the branches of the trees that lined the road. The leaves made shadowy patterns on the ground. Suraj tried hard not to think of his school report, but he knew that at any moment now the postman would be handing over a long brown envelope to his mother. He tried to imagine his mother's expression when she read the report; but the more he tried to picture her face, the more certain he was that, on knowing his result, she would show no expression at all. And having no expression on her face was much worse than having one.

Suraj heard the whistle of a train, and knew he was not far from the station. He cut through a field, climbed a hillock and ran down the slope until he was near the railway tracks. Here came the train, screeching and puffing: in the distance, a big black beetle, and then, when the carriages swung into sight, a centipede.

Suraj stood a good twenty metres away from the lines, on the slope of the hill. As the train passed, he pulled the handkerchief off his knee and began to wave it furiously. There was something about passing trains that filled him with awe and excitement. All those passengers, with mysterious lives and mysterious destinations, were people he wanted to know, people whose mysteries he wanted to unfold. He had been in a train recently, when his parents had taken him to bathe in the sacred river, Ganga, at Haridwar. He wished he could be in a train now; or, better still, be an engine-driver, with no more books and teachers and school reports. He did not know of any thirteen-year-old engine-drivers, but he saw himself driving the engine, shouting orders to the stoker; it made him feel powerful to be in control of a mighty steam-engine.

Someone—another boy—returned his wave, and the two waved at each other for a few seconds, and then the train had passed, its smoke spiralling backwards.

Suraj felt a little lonely now. Somehow, the passing of the train left him with a feeling of being alone in a wide, empty world. He was feeling hungry too. He went back to the field where he had seen some lichi trees, climbed into one of them and began plucking and peeling and eating the juicy red-skinned fruit. No one seemed to own the lichi trees because, although a dog appeared below and began barking, no one else appeared. Suraj kept spitting lichi seeds at the dog, and the dog kept barking at him. Eventually, the dog lost interest and slunk off.

Suraj began to feel drowsy in the afternoon heat. The lichi trees offered a lot of shade below, so he came down from the tree and sat on the grass, his back resting against the tree-trunk. A mynah-bird came hopping up to his feet and looked at him curiously, its head to one side.

Insects kept buzzing around Suraj. He swiped at them once or twice, but then couldn't make the effort to keep swiping. He opened his shirt buttons. The air was very hot, very still; the only sound was the faint buzzing of the insects. His head fell forward on his chest.

He opened his eyes to find himself being shaken, and looked up into the round, cheerful face of his friend Ranji.

'What are you doing, sleeping here?' asked Ranji, who was a couple of years younger than Suraj. 'Have you run away from home?'

'Not yet,' said Suraj. 'And what are you doing here?'

'Came for lichis.'

'So did I.'

They sat together for a while and talked and ate lichis. Then Ranji suggested that they visit the bazaar to eat fried pakoras.

'I haven't any money,' said Suraj.

'That doesn't matter,' said Ranji, who always seemed to be in funds. 'I have two rupees.'

So they walked to the bazaar. They crossed the field, walked back past the canal, skirted the maidaan, came to the clock tower and entered the bazaar.

The evening crowd had just begun to fill the road, and there was a lot of bustle and noise: the street-vendors called their wares in high, strident voices; children shouted and women bargained. There was a medley of smells and aromas coming from the little restaurants and sweet shops, and a medley of colours in the bangle and kite shops. Suraj and Ranji ate their pakoras, felt thirsty, and gazed at the rows and rows of coloured bottles at the cold drinks shop, where at least ten varieties of sweet, sticky, fizzy drinks were available. But they had already finished the two rupees, so there was nothing for them to do but quench their thirst at the municipal tap.

Afterwards they wandered down the crowded street, examining the shop-fronts, commenting on the passers-by, and every now and then greeting some friend or acquaintance.

Darkness came on suddenly, and then the bazaar was lit up, the big shops with bright electric and neon lights, the street-vendors with oil-lamps. The bazaar at night was even more exciting than during the day.

They traversed the bazaar from end to end, and when they were at the clock tower again, Ranji said he had to go home, and left Suraj. It was nearing Suraj's dinnertime and so, unwillingly, he too turned homewards. He did not want it to appear that he was deliberately staying out late because of the school report.

The lights were on in the front room when he got home. He waited outside, secure in the darkness of the verandah, watching the lighted room. His mother would be waiting for him, she would probably have the report in her hand or on the kitchen shelf, and she would have lots and lots of questions to ask him.

All the cares of the world seemed to descend on Suraj as he crept into the house.

'You're late,' said his mother. 'Come and have your food.'

Suraj said nothing, but removed his shoes outside the kitchen and sat down cross-legged on the kitchen floor, which was where he took his meals. He was tired and hungry. He no longer cared about anything.

'One of your class-fellows dropped in,' said his mother. 'He said your reports were sent out today. They'll arrive tomorrow.'

Tomorrow! Suraj felt a great surge of relief.

But then, just as suddenly, his spirits fell again.

Tomorrow…a further postponement of the dread moment, another night and another morning something would have to be done about it!

'Ma,' he said abruptly. 'Somi has asked me to his house again tomorrow.'

'I don't know how his mother puts up with you so often,' said Suraj's mother.

Suraj lay awake in bed, planning the morrow's activities: a game of cricket or football on the maidaan; perhaps a dip in the canal; a half-hour watching the trains thunder past; and in the evening an hour in the bazaar, among the kites and balloons and rose-coloured fizzy drinks and round dripping syrupy sweets... Perhaps, in the morning, he could persuade his mother to give him two or three rupees... It would be his last rupees for quite some time.

WHEN THE GUAVAS ARE RIPE

Guava trees are easy to climb. And guavas are good to eat. So it's little wonder that an orchard of guava trees is a popular place with boys and girls.

Just across the road from Ranji's house, on the other side of a low wall, was a large guava orchard. The monsoon rains were almost over. It was a warm, humid day in September, and the guavas were ripening, turning from green to gold; no longer hard, but growing soft and sweet and juicy.

The schools were closed because of a religious festival. Ranji's father was at work in his office. Ranji's mother was enjoying an afternoon siesta on a cot in the backyard. His grandmother was busy teaching her pet parrot to recite a prayer.

'I feel like getting into those guava trees,' said Ranji to himself. 'It's months since I climbed a tree.'

He was soon across the road and over the wall and among the trees. He chose a tree that grew in the middle of the orchard, where it was unlikely that he would be disturbed; then he climbed swiftly into its branches. A cluster of guavas swung just above him. He reached up for one of them, but to his surprise he found himself clutching a small, bare foot which had suddenly been thrust through the foliage.

Having caught the foot, Ranji did not let go. Instead he pulled hard on it. There was a squeal and someone came toppling down on him. Ranji found himself clutching at arms and legs. Together they crashed through a couple of branches and landed with a thud on the soft ground beneath the tree.

Ranji and the intruder struggled fiercely. They rolled about on the grass. Ranji tried a judo hold—without any success. Then he saw that his opponent was a girl. It was his friend and neighbour, Koki.

'It's you!' he gasped.

'It's me,' said Koki. 'And what are *you* doing here?'

'Get your knee out of my stomach and I'll tell you.'

When he had recovered his breath, he said, 'I just felt like climbing a tree.'

'So did I.'

He stared at her. There was guava juice at the corners of her mouth and on her chin.

'Are the guavas good?' he asked.

'Quite sweet, in this tree,' said Koki. 'You find another tree for yourself, Ranji. There must be thirty or forty trees to choose from.'

'And all going to waste,' said Ranji. 'Look, some of the guavas have been spoilt by the birds.'

'Nobody wants them, it seems.'

Koki climbed back onto her tree, and Ranji obligingly walked a little further and climbed another tree. After a few polite exchanges they fell silent, their attention given over entirely to the eating of guavas.

'I've eaten five,' said Koki after some time.

'You'd better stop.'

'You're only saying that because you've just started.'

'Well, three's enough for me.'

'I'm getting a tummy ache, I think.'

'I warned you. Come on, I'll take you home. We can come back tomorrow. There are still lots of guavas left.'

'I don't think I want to eat any more,' said Koki.

◆

She felt better the next day—so well, in fact, that Ranji found her leaning on the gate, waiting for him to join her. She was accompanied by her small brother, Teju, who was only six and very mischievous.

'How are you feeling today?' asked Ranji.

'Hungry,' said Koki.

'Why did you bring your brother?'

'He wants to start climbing trees.'

Soon they were in the orchard. Ranji and Koki helped Teju onto the branches of one of the smaller trees and then made for other trees, disturbing a party of parrots who flew in circles around the orchard, screaming their protests.

Two boys and a girl talking to each other from three different trees can make quite a lot of noise, and it wasn't only the birds who were disturbed. Though they did not know it, the orchard belonged to a wealthy property dealer and he employed a watchman, whose duty it was to keep away birds, children, monkeys, flying foxes, and other fruit-eating pests. But on a hot, sultry afternoon, Gopal, the watchman, could not resist taking a nap. He was stretched out under a shady jackfruit tree, snoring so loudly that the flies who had been buzzing around him felt that a storm was brewing and kept their distance.

He woke to the sound of voices raised high in glee. Sitting up, he brushed a ladybird from his long moustache, then seized his lathi, a long, stout stick usually carried by watchmen.

'Who's there?' he shouted, struggling to his feet.

There was a sudden silence on the trees.

'Who's there?' he called again.

No answer.

'I must have been dreaming,' he muttered, and was preparing to lie down and take another nap when Teju, who had been watching him, burst into laughter.

'Ho!' shouted the watchman, coming to life again. 'Thieves! I'll settle you!' And he began striding towards the centre of the orchard, boasting all the time of his physical prowess. 'I'm not afraid of thieves, bandits, or wild beasts! I'll have you know that I was once the wrestling champion of the entire district of Dehra. Come on out and fight me if you dare!'

'Run!' hissed Koki, scrambling down from her tree.

'Run!' shouted Ranji, as though it were a cricket match.

Teju was so startled by the sudden activity that he tumbled out of his tree and began crying and Ranji and Koki had to go to his aid.

The sight of an enormous ex-wrestler bearing down on them was enough to make Teju stop crying and get to his feet. Then all three were fleeing across the grove, the watchman a little way behind them, waving his lathi and shouting at the top of his voice. Although he was an ex-wrestler (or perhaps because of it) he could not run very fast and was still huffing and puffing some twenty metres behind them when they climbed up and over the wall. He could not climb walls either. They ran off in different directions before returning home.

◆

Next day, Ranji met Koki and Teju at the far end of the road.

'Is he there?' asked Koki.

'I haven't seen him. But he must be around somewhere.'

'Maybe he's gone for his lunch. We'll just walk past and take a quick look.'

The three of them strolled casually down the road. Koki said the gardens were looking very pretty. Teju gazed admiringly at a boy flying a kite from a rooftop. Ranji kept one eye on the road and one eye on the orchard wall. A squirrel ran along the top of the wall; the parrots were back in the guava trees.

They moved closer to the wall. Ranji leaned casually against it and Koki began to pick little daisies growing at the edge of the road. Teju, unable to hide his curiosity, pulled himself up on the wall and looked over. At the same time, Gopal, the watchman, who had been hiding behind the wall waiting for them, stood up slowly and glared fiercely at Teju.

Teju gulped, but he did not flinch. He was looking straight into the watchman's red angry eyes.

'And what can I do for you?' growled Gopal.

'I was just looking,' said Teju.

'At what?'

'At the view.'

Gopal was a little baffled. They looked just like the children he'd chased away yesterday, but he couldn't be sure. They didn't *look* guilty. But did children ever look guilty?

'There's a better view from the other side of the road,' he said gruffly. 'Now be off!'

'What lovely guavas,' said Koki, smiling sweetly. There

weren't many people who could resist that smile!

'True,' said Ranji, with the air of one who was an expert on guavas and all things good to eat. 'They are just the right size and colour. I don't think I've seen better. But they'll be spoilt by the birds if you don't gather them soon.'

'It's none of your business,' said the watchman.

'Just look at his muscles,' said Teju, trying a different approach. 'He's really strong!'

Gopal looked pleased for once. He was proud of his former prowess, even though he was now rather flabby around the waist.

'You look like a wrestler,' said Ranji.

'I *am* a wrestler,' said Gopal.

'I told you so,' said Koki. 'What else could he be?'

'I'm a retired wrestler,' said Gopal.

'You don't look retired,' said Teju, fast learning that flattery can get you almost anywhere.

Gopal swelled with pride; such admiration hadn't come his way for a long time. To Koki he looked like a bullfrog swelling up, but she thought it better not to say so.

'Do you want to see my muscles?' he asked.

'Yes, yes!' they cried. 'Do show us!'

Gopal peeled off his shirt and thumped his chest. It sounded like a drum. They were really impressed. Then he bent his elbow and his biceps bulged like cricket balls.

'You can touch them,' he said generously.

Teju poked a finger into Gopal's biceps.

'Mister Universe!' he exclaimed.

Gopal glowed all over. He liked these children. How intelligent they were! Not everyone had the sense to appreciate his strength, his manliness, his magnificent physique!

'Climb over the wall and join me,' he said. 'Come sit on

the grass and I'll tell you about the time when I was a wrestling champion.'

Over the wall they came and sat politely on the grass. Gopal told them about some of his exploits: how he had vanquished a world-famous wrestler in five seconds flat, and how he had saved a carload of travellers from drowning by single-handedly dragging their car out of a river. They listened patiently. Then Teju mentioned that he was feeling hungry.

'Hungry?' said Gopal. 'Why didn't you tell me before? I'll bring you some guavas, that's all there is to eat here. I know which tree has the best ones. And they're all going to rot if no one eats them—no one's buying the crop this year, the owner's price is too high!'

Gopal hurried off and soon returned with a basket full of guavas.

'Help yourselves,' he said. 'But don't eat too many, you'll get sick.'

So they munched guavas and listened to Gopal tell them about the time he was waylaid by three bandits and how he threw them all into the village pond.

'Will you come again tomorrow?' asked Gopal eagerly, when the guavas were finished and the children got up to leave. 'Come tomorrow and I'll tell you another story.'

'We'll come tomorrow,' said Teju, looking at all the guava trees still laden with fruit.

Somehow it seemed very important to Gopal that they should come again. It was lonely in the orchard. Koki sensed this and said, 'We like your stories.'

'They are good stories,' said Ranji, even if they were not entirely true, he thought...

They climbed over the wall and waved goodbye to Gopal.

They came again the next day.

And even when the guava season was over and Gopal had nothing to offer them but his stories, they went to see him because by that time they had grown to like him.

KOKI PLAYS THE GAME

'There's a cricket match on Saturday, isn't there?' asked Koki.
'That's right,' said Ranji. 'We're playing the Public School team.'

'I might come and watch,' said Koki.

'As you like. It won't be much of a game. We'll beat them easily.'

Ranji's own cricket team was quite different from his school team. It consisted of boys big and small, long and short, from various walks of life. Even Koki, a girl, was allowed honorary membership, and had sometimes been 'twelfth man'—an extra. She knew the game well, and often bowled to Ranji in the mornings when he wanted batting practice. Only a couple of the teammates could afford to go to private schools like Ranji's; most of them went to the local government school, and two or three had stopped going to school altogether.

There was Bhartu, who delivered newspapers in the mornings; the brothers Mukesh and Rakesh, whose father kept a sweet shop; and a tailor's son, Amir Ali. There was Billy

Jones, an Anglo-Indian boy; 'Lumboo', the Tall One; Sitaram, the washerman's son, and several others. And there was also Bhim, who couldn't play at all, but who made a good umpire (when his glasses weren't steamed over) and who accompanied the team wherever it went.

This Saturday they were playing on their 'home' ground, a patch of wasteland behind a new cinema called the Apsara ('Heavenly Dancer').

The Public School boys had all arrived first, which was only natural since they lived together in the same boarding school. The members of Ranji's team came from different directions, so it was some time before they had all assembled. Even then, they were two short. But Ranji won the toss and decided to bat, hoping that the missing team members would arrive in time to take their turn at the wicket.

'If Mukesh and Rakesh aren't here in time, we won't have them in the team,' said Ranji sternly.

'Don't sack them,' said Lumboo. 'They always bring us sweets and snacks from their father's shop. We need them in the team even if they don't score any runs.'

'Well, if they turn up *without* refreshments, they'll be sacked,' said Ranji, always ready to be fair.

The two umpires had gone out to set up the stumps—Bhim, on behalf of Ranji's team, and a teacher from the Public School.

'I don't like the look of that teacher,' said Amir Ali.

'Well, we won't take any risks.'

Billy Jones and Lumboo always opened the batting. Lumboo's height helped him to deal with the fast-rising ball. He took the first ball.

The Public School's opening bowler was speedy but inaccurate. This was because he was trying to bowl too fast.

His first ball went for a wide, which gave Ranji's team its first run. The second ball wasn't quite so wide, but it was still about a foot from the leg stump. Lumboo took a swipe at it and missed. The third ball pitched halfway down the wicket and kept low. It struck Lumboo on the pads.

'How's that!' shouted the bowler, wicketkeeper and slip-fielders in unison.

The Public School's umpire did not hesitate. Up went his finger. Lumboo was given out leg-before-wicket. Lumboo stood aghast. He looked down at where his feet were placed, then back at his stumps.

'I'm not in front of the wicket,' he complained to no one in particular.

'The umpire's word is law,' said the wicketkeeper.

Lumboo slowly walked back to where his teammates reclined against a pile of bricks.

'I wasn't out!' he protested.

'Never mind,' said Ranji, whose turn it was to bat. 'You'll get your chance when you come on to bowl.'

He walked to the wicket with a confident air, his bat resting on his shoulder. He took guard carefully and, tapping his bat on the ground, faced the bowler. He received a straight ball, fast, and met it on the half-volley, driving it straight back past the bowler. It sped to the boundary, amidst delighted cries from Ranji's teammates. Four runs.

The next ball was short, just outside the off stump. Ranji stepped back and square-cut it past point. Another four. There were more cheers, and this time Ranji distinctly heard a girl's voice shouting: 'Good shot, Ranji!'

He looked back to where his teammates were gathered. There was no girl among them. He turned and looked towards the opposite boundary, and there, under the giant cinema hoarding, stood Koki. She waved to him.

Ranji did not wave back. He felt acutely self-conscious. Settling down to face the bowler again, he was aware of two things at once—of the bowler making faces and charging up to bowl, and of Koki standing on the boundary and waiting for him to hit another four.

This loss of concentration caused him to misjudge the next ball. Instead of playing forward, he played back.

The ball took the edge of his bat and flew straight into the wicketkeeper's gloves.

'How's that!' shouted all the fielders, appealing for a catch.

Ranji did not wait for the umpire—in this case, Bhim, to give him out. He knew he'd touched the ball. Scowling, he walked back to his team. It was all Koki's fault!

Now, there was a good partnership between Sitaram and Bhartu. Sitaram, who helped his father with the town's washing on Sundays, was in the habit of laying out clothes on a flat stone and pounding them with a stout stick—the method followed by most washermen.

He dealt with the cricket ball in much the same way—clouting it hard, and sending it to various points of the compass. He hit up 25 valuable runs before he was out, caught off a big hit. Bhartu pushed and prodded, merely keeping one end going, until he too was out to an LBW decision. Billy Jones had gone the same way, taking the ball on his pads. No one was happy with the LBW decisions.

'We must have neutral umpires,' said Amir Ali.

'But who wants to be an umpire?' said Ranji. 'We won't find anyone. We'll have to use our own team members—or let the other side provide *both* umpires!'

'Not after today,' said Lumboo.

Meanwhile, Mukesh and Rakesh had arrived, carrying paper bags full of samosas and jalebis. As a result, everyone cheered up. Wickets fell almost as rapidly as the snacks and sweets were consumed. Mukesh and Rakesh, who were the last men in, held out for several overs until Rakesh was given out—LBW! Ranji's team was all out for 87 runs—not really a match-winning score, except on a tricky wicket.

It was the Public School team's turn to bat. One of their opening batsmen was bowled by Lumboo for naught. The other batsman was twice rapped on the pads by balls from Ranji, but his loud appeals for LBW were turned down—by the Public School's umpire, naturally! Muttering to himself, Ranji hurled down a thunderbolt of a ball. It rose sharply and struck the batsman on the hand. Howling with pain, he dropped his bat and wrung his hand. Then he showed everyone a swollen finger and decided to 'retire hurt'.

'There's more than one way of getting them out,' muttered Ranji, as he passed the umpire.

The next two batsmen were good players, not as nervous as the openers. One of them got what might have been a faint tickle to an out-swinger from Lumboo, but he was given the benefit of the doubt by Bhim—who, as umpires went, was as impartial as a star. He showed no favours to his own team, no matter what the other umpire did. It just isn't fair, thought Ranji.

The number three and four batsmen put on 40 runs between them, and by mid-afternoon Ranji's players were feeling tired and hungry. Then three quick wickets fell to Sitaram's spinners. Three wickets remained, and 20 runs were needed by the Public School for victory.

This was when Bhartu, running to take a catch, collided

with chubby Mukesh. Both of them went sprawling on the grass, and when they got up the ball was found lodged in the back of Mukesh's pants. How it got there no one could tell, but after much discussion the umpires had to agree that it qualified as a catch and the batsman was given out. But Bhartu had to leave the ground with a bleeding nose.

Ranji looked around for a replacement. There was no one in sight except Koki.

'Come and field,' said Ranji brusquely.

Koki needed no persuading. She slipped off her sandals and dashed barefoot on to the field, taking up Bhartu's position near the boundary.

The tail-end batsmen were now swinging at the ball in a desperate attempt to hit the remaining runs. A hard-hit drive sped past Koki and went for four runs. Ranji gave her a hard look. Then the two batsmen got into a muddle while trying to take a quick run, and one of them was run out.

The last man came in. The Public School was 8 runs behind. But a couple of boundaries would take care of that.

The batsmen ran two. And then one of them, over-confident and sure of victory, swung out at a slow, tempting ball from Sitaram, and the ball flew towards Koki in a long, curving arc.

Koki had to run a few yards to her left. Then she leapt like a gazelle and took the ball in both hands. Ranji's team had won, and Koki had made the winning catch.

It was her last appearance as 'twelfth man'. From that day onwards she was a regular member of the team.

HOME

'The boy's useless,' said Mr Kapoor, speaking to his wife but making sure his son could hear. 'I don't know what he'll do with himself when he grows up. He takes no interest in his studies.'

Suraj's father had returned from a business trip and was seeing his son's school report for the first time. 'Good at cricket,' said the report. 'Poor in studies. Does not pay attention in class.'

Suraj's mother, a quiet, dignified woman, said nothing. Suraj stood at the window, refusing to speak. He stared out at the light drizzle that whispered across the garden. He had angry black eyes and bushy eyebrows, and he was feeling rebellious.

His father was doing all the talking. 'What's the use of spending money on his education if he can't show anything for it? He comes home, eats as much as three boys, asks for money, and then goes out to loaf with his friends!'

Mr Kapoor paused, expecting Suraj to reply and give cause for further scolding; but Suraj knew that silence would irritate his father even more, and there were times when he enjoyed watching his father get irritated.

'Well, I won't stand for it,' said Mr Kapoor finally. 'If you don't make some effort, my boy, you can leave this house!' And having at last addressed Suraj directly, he stormed out of the room.

Suraj remained a few moments at the window. Then he went to the front door, opened it, stepped out into the rain, and banged the door behind him.

His mother made as if to call out after him, but she thought better of it, and turned and walked into the kitchen.

Suraj stood in the drizzle, looking back at the house.

'I'll never go back,' he said fiercely. 'I can manage without them. If they want me back, they can come and ask me to return!'

And he thrust his hands into his pockets and walked down the road with an independent air.

His fingers came into contact with a familiar crispness, a five rupee note. It was all the money he had in the world. He clutched it tight. He had meant to spend it at the cinema, but now it would have to serve more urgent needs. He wasn't sure what these needs would be because just now he was angry and his mind wasn't running on practical lines. He walked blindly, unconscious of the rain, until he reached the maidaan.

When he reached the maidaan, the sun came out.

Though there was still a drizzle, the sun seemed to raise Suraj's spirits at once. He remembered his friend Ranji and decided he would stay with Ranji until he found some sort of work. He knew that if he didn't find work, he wouldn't be able to stay away from home for long. He wondered what kind of work a thirteen-year-old could get. He did not fancy delivering newspapers or serving tea in a small tea shop in the bazaar; it was much better being a customer.

The drizzle ceased altogether, and Suraj hurried across the maidaan and down a quiet road until he reached Ranji's house. When he went in at the gate, his spirits sank.

The house was shut. There was a lock on the front door. Suraj went round the house three times but he couldn't find an open door or window. Perhaps, he thought, the family have gone out for the morning—a picnic or birthday treat; they were sure to be back for lunch. With spirits mounting once again, he strolled leisurely down the road, in the direction of the bazaar.

Suraj had a weakness for the bazaar, for its crowded variety of goods, its smells and colours and the music playing over the loudspeakers. He lingered now at a tea-and-pakora shop, tempted by the appetizing smells that came from inside; but decided that he would eat at Ranji's house and spend his money on something other than food. He couldn't resist the big yellow yo-yo in the toy-seller's glass case; it was set with pieces of different shine, coloured glass which shone and twinkled in the sunshine.

'How much?' asked Suraj.

'Two rupees,' said the shop-keeper. 'But to a regular customer like you I give it for one rupee.'

'It must be an old one,' said Suraj, but he paid the rupee and took possession of the yo-yo. He immediately began working it, strolling through the bazaar with the yo-yo swinging up and down from his index finger.

Fingering the four remaining notes in his pocket, he decided that he was thirsty. Not tap-water, nor a fizzy drink, but only a vanilla milkshake would meet his need. He sat at a table and sucked milkshake through a straw. One eye caught sight of the clock on the wall. It was nearly one o'clock. Ranji and his family should be home by now.

Suraj slipped off his chair, paid for the drink—that left him with two rupees—and went sauntering down the bazaar road, the yo-yo making soothing sounds beside him.

Ranji's house was still shut.

This was something Suraj hadn't anticipated. He walked quickly round the house, but it was locked as before. On his second round he met the gardener, an old man over sixty.

'Where is everybody?' asked Suraj.

'They have gone to Delhi for a week,' said the gardener, looking sharply at Suraj. 'Why, is anything the matter?'

Suraj had never seen the old man before, but he did not hesitate to confide in him. 'I've left home. I was going to stay with Ranji. Now there's nowhere to go.'

The old man thought this over for a minute. His face was wrinkled like a walnut, his hands and feet hard and cracked; but his eyes were bright and almost youthful.

He was a part-time gardener, who worked for several families along the road; there were no big gardens in this part of the town.

'Why don't you go home again?' he suggested.

'It's too soon,' said Suraj. 'I haven't really run away as yet. They must know I've run away. Then they'll feel sorry!'

The gardener smiled. 'You should have planned it better,' he said. 'Have you saved any money?' 'I had five rupees this morning. Now there are two rupees left.' He looked down at his yo-yo. 'Would you like to buy it?'

'I wouldn't know how to work it,' said the gardener. 'The best thing for you to do is to go home, wait till Ranji gets back, and then run away.'

Suraj considered this interesting advice, and decided that

there was something in it. But he didn't make up his mind right away. A little suspense at home would be a good thing for his parents.

He returned to the maidaan and sat down on the grass. As soon as he sat down, he felt hungry.

He had never felt so hungry before. Visions of tandoori chickens and dripping spangled sweets danced before him. He wondered if the toy-seller would take back the yo-yo. He probably would, for half the price; but, as much as Suraj wanted food, he did not want to give up the yo-yo.

There was nothing to do but go home. His mother, he was sure, would be worried by now. His father (he hoped) would be pacing up and down the verandah, glancing at his watch every few seconds. It would be a lesson to them. He would walk back into the house as if doing them a favour.

He only hoped they had kept his lunch.

Suraj walked into the sitting-room and threw his yoyo on the sofa.

Mr Kapoor was sitting in his favourite armchair, reading a newspaper prior to going back to his office. He stood up for a moment as Suraj came into the room, said, 'You're very late,' and returned to his newspaper.

Suraj found his mother and his food in the kitchen. She did not speak to him, but was smiling to herself.

'Feeling hungry?' she asked.

'No,' said Suraj, and seized the tray and tucked into his food.

When he returned to the sitting-room he was surprised to see his father fumbling with the yo-yo.

'How do you work this stupid thing?' said Mr Kapoor.

Suraj didn't reply. He just stood there gloating over his father's clumsiness. At last he couldn't help bursting into laughter.

'It's easy,' he said. 'I'll show you.' And he took the yo-yo from his father and gave a demonstration.

When Mrs Kapoor came into the room she did not appear at all surprised to find her husband and son deeply absorbed in the working of a cheap bazaar toy. She was used to such absurdities. Men never really grew up.

Mr Kapoor had forgotten he was supposed to be returning to his office, and Suraj had forgotten about running away. They had both forgotten the morning's unpleasantness. That had been a long, long time ago.

THE PLAYING FIELDS OF SHIMLA

It had been a lonely winter for a twelve-year-old boy.

I hadn't really got over my father's untimely death two years previously; nor had I as yet reconciled myself to my mother's marriage to the Punjabi gentleman who dealt in second-hand cars. The three-month winter break over, I was almost happy to return to my boarding school in Shimla—that elegant hill station once celebrated by Kipling and soon to lose its status as the summer capital of the Raj in India.

It wasn't as though I had many friends at school. I had always been a bit of a loner, shy and reserved, looking out only for my father's rare visits—on his brief leaves from RAF duties—and to my sharing his tent or air force hutment outside Delhi or Karachi. Those unsettled but happy days would not come again. I needed a friend but it was not easy to find one among a horde of rowdy, pea-shooting fourth formers, who carved their names on desks and stuck chewing gum on the class teacher's chair. Had I grown up with other children, I might have developed a taste for schoolboy anarchy; but, in sharing my father's loneliness after his separation from my mother, I had turned into a premature adult. The mixed nature of my reading—Dickens, Richmal Crompton, Tagore and *Champion* and *Film Fun* comics—probably reflected the confused state of my life. A book reader was rare even in those pre-electronic times. On rainy days most boys played cards or Monopoly, or listened to Artie Shaw on the wind-up gramophone in the common room.

After a month in the fourth form I began to notice a new boy, Omar, and then only because he was a quiet, almost taciturn person who took no part in the form's feverish attempts to imitate the Marx Brothers at the circus. He showed no resentment at the prevailing anarchy, nor did he make a move to participate in it. Once he caught me looking at him, and he smiled ruefully, tolerantly. Did I sense another adult in the class? Someone who was a little older than his years?

Even before we began talking to each other, Omar and I developed an understanding of sorts, and we'd nod almost respectfully to each other when we met in the classroom corridors or the environs of dining hall or dormitory. We were not in the same house. The house system practised its own form of apartheid, whereby a member of, say, Curzon House was not expected to fraternize with someone belonging to Rivaz or Lefroy! Those public schools certainly knew how to clamp you into compartments. However, these barriers vanished when Omar and I found ourselves selected for the School Colts' hockey team—Omar as a fullback, I as goalkeeper. I think a defensive position suited me by nature. In all modesty I have to say that I made a good goalkeeper, both at hockey and football. And fifty years on, I am still keeping goal. Then I did it between goalposts, now I do it off the field—protecting a family, protecting my independence as a writer...

The taciturn Omar now spoke to me occasionally, and we combined well on the field of play. A good understanding is needed between goalkeeper and fullback. We were on the same wavelength. I anticipated his moves, he was familiar with mine. Years later, when I read Conrad's *The Secret Sharer,* I thought of Omar.

It wasn't until we were away from the confines of school, classroom and dining hall that our friendship flourished. The hockey team travelled to Sanawar on the next mountain range, where we were to play a couple of matches against our old rivals, the Lawrence Royal Military School. This had been my father's old school, but I did not know that in his time it had also been a military orphanage. Grandfather, who had been a private foot soldier—of the likes of Kipling's Mulvaney, Otheris and Learoyd—had joined the Scottish Rifles after leaving home at the age of seventeen. He had died while his children were still very young, but my father's more rounded education had enabled him to become an officer.

Omar and I were thrown together a good deal during the visit to Sanawar, and in our more leisurely moments, strolling undisturbed around a school where we were guests and not pupils, we exchanged life histories and other confidences. Omar, too, had lost his father—had I sensed that before?—shot in some tribal encounter on the Frontier, for he hailed from the lawless lands beyond Peshawar. A wealthy uncle was seeing to Omar's education. The RAF was now seeing to mine.

We wandered into the school chapel, and there I found my father's name—A.A. Bond—on the school's roll of honour board: old boys who had lost their lives while serving during the two World Wars.

'What did his initials stand for?' asked Omar.

'Aubrey Alexander.'

'Unusual names, like yours. Why did your parents call you Ruskin?'

'I am not sure. I think my father liked the works of John Ruskin, who wrote on serious subjects like art and architecture. I don't think anyone reads him now. They'll read me, though!' I had already started writing my first book. It was called *Nine Months* (the length of the school term, not a pregnancy), and it described some of the happenings at school and lampooned a few of our teachers. I had filled three slim exercise books with this premature literary project, and I allowed Omar to go through them. He must have been my first reader and critic. 'They're very interesting,' he said, 'but you'll get into trouble if someone finds them. Especially Mr Oliver.' And he read out an offending verse—

Olly, Olly, Olly, with his balls on a trolley,
And his arse all painted green!

I have to admit it wasn't great literature. I was better at hockey and football. I made some spectacular saves, and we won our matches against Sanawar. When we returned to Shimla, we were school heroes for a couple of days and lost some of our reticence; we were even a little more forthcoming with other boys. And then Mr Fisher, my housemaster, discovered my literary opus, *Nine Months,* under my mattress, and took it away and read it (as he told me later) from cover to cover. Corporal punishment then being in vogue, I was given six of the best with a springy malacca cane, and my manuscript was torn up and deposited in Fisher's waste-paper basket. All I had to show for my efforts were some purple welts on my bottom. These were proudly displayed to all who were interested, and I was a hero for another two days.

'Will you go away too when the British leave India?' Omar asked me one day.

'I don't think so,' I said. 'My stepfather is Indian.'

'Everyone is saying that our leaders and the British are going to divide the country. Shimla will be in India, Peshawar in Pakistan!'

'Oh, it won't happen,' I said glibly. 'How can they cut up such a big country?' But even as we chatted about the possibility, Nehru and Jinnah and Mountbatten and all those who mattered were preparing their instruments for major surgery.

Before their decision impinged on our lives and everyone else's, we found a little freedom of our own—in an underground tunnel that we discovered below the third flat.

It was really part of an old, disused drainage system, and when Omar and I began exploring it, we had no idea just how far it extended. After crawling along on our bellies for some twenty feet, we found ourselves in complete darkness. Omar had brought along a small pencil torch, and with its help we continued writhing forward (moving backwards would have been quite impossible) until we saw a glimmer of light at the end of the tunnel. Dusty, musty, very scruffy, we emerged at last on to a grassy knoll, a little way outside the school boundary.

It's always a great thrill to escape beyond the boundaries that adults have devised. Here we were in unknown territory. To travel without passports—that would be the ultimate in freedom!

But more passports were on their way and more boundaries.

Lord Mountbatten, Viceroy and Governor-General-to-be, came for our Founder's Day and gave away the prizes. I had won a prize for something or the other, and mounted the rostrum to receive my book from this towering, handsome man in his pinstripe suit. Bishop Cotton's was then the premier school of India, often referred to as the 'Eton of the East'. Viceroys and Governors had graced its functions. Many of its boys had gone on to eminence in the civil services and armed forces. There was one 'old boy' about whom they maintained a stolid silence— General Dyer, who had ordered the massacre at Amritsar and destroyed the trust that had been building up between Britain and India.

Now Mountbatten spoke of the momentous events that were happening all around us—the War had just come to an end, the United Nations held out the promise of a world living in peace and harmony, and India, an equal partner with Britain, would be among the great nations...

A few weeks later, Bengal and Punjab provinces were bisected. Riots flared up across northern India, and there was a great exodus of people crossing the newly drawn frontiers of Pakistan and India. Homes were destroyed, thousands lost their lives.

The common-room radio and the occasional newspaper kept us abreast of events, but in our tunnel, Omar and I felt immune from all that was happening, worlds away from all the pillage, murder and revenge. And outside the tunnel, on the pine knoll below the school, there was fresh untrodden grass, sprinkled with clover and daisies, the only sounds the hammering of a woodpecker, the distant insistent call of the Himalayan barbet. Who could touch us there?

'And when all the wars are done,' I said, 'a butterfly will still be beautiful.'

'Did you read that somewhere?'

'No, it just came into my head.'

'Already you're a writer.'

'No, I want to play hockey for India or football for Arsenal. Only winning teams!'

'You can't win forever. Better to be a writer.'

When the monsoon rains arrived, the tunnel was flooded, the drain choked with rubble. We were allowed out to the cinema to see Lawrence Olivier's *Hamlet,* a film that did nothing to raise our spirits on a wet and gloomy afternoon—but it was our last picture that year, because communal riots suddenly broke out in Shimla's Lower Bazaar, an area that was still much as Kipling had described it—'a man who knows his way there can defy all the police of India's summer capital'—and we were confined to school indefinitely.

One morning after chapel, the headmaster announced that the Muslim boys—those who had their homes in what was now Pakistan—would have to be evacuated, sent to their homes across the border with an armed convoy.

The tunnel no longer provided an escape for us. The bazaar was out of bounds. The flooded playing field was deserted. Omar and I sat on a damp wooden bench and talked about the future in vaguely hopeful terms; but we didn't solve any problems. Mountbatten and Nehru and Jinnah were doing all the solving.

It was soon time for Omar to leave—he along with some fifty other boys from Lahore, Pindi and Peshawar. The rest of us—Hindus, Christians, Parsis—helped them load their luggage into the waiting trucks. A couple of boys broke down and wept. So did our departing school captain, a Pathan who had been known for his stoic and unemotional demeanour. Omar waved cheerfully to me and I waved back. We had vowed to meet again some day,

The convoy got through safely enough. There was only one

casualty—the school cook, who had strayed into an off-limits area in the foothill town of Kalka and been set upon by a mob. He wasn't seen again.

Towards the end of the school year, just as we were all getting ready to leave for the school holidays, I received a letter from Omar. He told me something about his new school and how he missed my company and our games and our tunnel to freedom. I replied and gave him my home address, but I did not hear from him again. The land, though divided, was still a big one, and we were very small.

Some seventeen or eighteen years later I did get news of Omar, but in an entirely different context. India and Pakistan were at war and in a bombing raid over Ambala, not far from Shimla, a Pakistani plane was shot down. Its crew died in the crash. One of them, I learnt later, was Omar.

Did he, I wonder, get a glimpse of the playing fields we knew so well as boys?

Perhaps memories of his schooldays flooded back as he flew over the foothills. Perhaps he remembered the tunnel through which we were able to make our little escape to freedom.

But there are no tunnels in the sky.

CHILDREN OF INDIA

They pass me every day, on their way to school—boys and girls from the surrounding villages and the outskirts of the hill station. There are no school buses plying for these children: they walk.

For many of them, it's a very long walk to school.

Ranbir, who is ten, has to climb the mountain from his village, four miles distant and 2,000 feet below the town level. He comes in all weathers, wearing the same pair of cheap shoes until they have almost fallen apart.

Ranbir is a cheerful soul. He waves to me whenever he sees me at my window. Sometimes he brings me cucumbers from his father's field. I pay him for the cucumbers; he uses the money for books or for small things needed at home.

Many of the children are like Ranbir—poor, but slightly better off than what their parents were at the same age. They cannot attend the expensive residential and private schools that abound here, but must go to the government-aided schools with only basic facilities. Not many of their parents managed to go to school. They spent their lives working in the fields or delivering milk in the hill station. The lucky ones got into the army. Perhaps Ranbir will do something different when he grows up.

He has yet to see a train but he sees planes flying over the mountains almost every day.

'How far can a plane go?' he asks.

'All over the world,' I tell him. 'Thousands of miles in a day. You can go almost anywhere.'

'I'll go round the world one day,' he vows. 'I'll buy a plane and go everywhere!'

And maybe he will. He has a determined chin and a defiant look in his eye.

The following lines in my journal were put down for my own inspiration or encouragement, but they will do for any determined young person:

> We get out of life what we bring to it. There is not a dream which may not come true if we have the energy which determines our own fate. We can always get what we want if we will it intensely enough...So few people succeed greatly because so few people conceive a great end, working towards it without giving up. We all know that the man who works steadily for money gets rich; the man who works day and night for fame or power reaches his goal. And those who work for deeper, more spiritual achievements will find them too. It may come when we no longer have any use for it, but if we have been willing it long enough, it will come!

◆

Up to a few years ago, very few girls in the hills or in the villages of India went to school. They helped in the home until they were old enough to be married, which wasn't very old. But there are now just as many girls as there are boys going to school.

Bindra is something of an extrovert—a confident fourteen-year-old who chatters away as she hurries down the road with her companions. Her father is a forest guard and knows me quite well: I meet him on my walks through the deodar woods behind Landour. And I had grown used to seeing Bindra almost every day. When she did not put in an appearance for a week, I asked her brother if anything was wrong.

'Oh, nothing,' he says, 'she is helping my mother cut grass. Soon the monsoon will end and the grass will dry up. So we cut it now and store it for the cows for winter.'

'And why aren't you cutting grass, too?'

'Oh, I have a cricket match today,' he says, and hurries away to join his team-mates. Unlike his sister, he puts pleasure before work!

Cricket, once the game of the elite, has become the game of the masses. On any holiday, in any part of this vast country, groups of boys can be seen making their way to the nearest field, or open patch of land, with bat, ball and any other cricketing gear that they can cobble together. Watching some of them play, I am amazed at the quality of talent, at the finesse with which they bat or bowl. Some of the local teams are as good, if not better, than any from the private schools, where there are better facilities. But the boys from these poor or lower-middle-class families will never get the exposure that is necessary to bring them to the attention of those who select state or national teams. They will never get near enough to the men of influence and power. They must continue to play for the love of the game, or watch their more fortunate heroes' exploits on television.

◆

As winter approaches and the days grow shorter, those children who live far away must quicken their pace in order to get home before dark. Ranbir and his friends find that darkness has fallen before they are halfway home.

'What is the time, Uncle?' he asks, as he trudges up the steep road past Ivy Cottage.

One gets used to being called 'Uncle' by almost every boy or girl one meets. I wonder how the custom began. Perhaps it has its origins in the folk tale about the tiger who refrained from pouncing on you if you called him 'uncle'. Tigers don't eat their relatives! Or do they? The ploy may not work if the tiger happens to be a tigress. Would you call her 'Aunty' as she (or your teacher!) descends on you?

It's dark at six and by then, Ranbir likes to be out of the deodar forest and on the open road to the village. The moon and the stars and the village lights are sufficient, but not in the forest, where it is dark even during the day. And the silent flitting of bats and flying foxes, and the eerie hoot of an owl, can be a little disconcerting for the hardiest of children. Once Ranbir and the other boys were chased by a bear.

When he told me about it, I said, 'Well, now we know you can run faster than a bear!'

'Yes, but you have to run downhill when chased by a bear.' He spoke as one having long experience of escaping from bears. 'They run much faster uphill!'

'I'll remember that,' I said, 'thanks for the advice.' And I don't suppose calling a bear 'Uncle' would help.

Usually Ranbir has the company of other boys, and they

sing most of the way, for loud singing by small boys will silence owls and frighten away the forest demons. One of them plays a flute, and flute music in the mountains is always enchanting.

◆

Not only in the hills, but all over India, children are constantly making their way to and from school, in conditions that range from dust storms in the Rajasthan desert to blizzards in Ladakh and Kashmir. In the larger towns and cities, there are school buses, but in remote rural areas getting to school can pose a problem.

Most children are more than equal to any obstacles that may arise. Like those youngsters in the Ganjam district of Orissa. In the absence of a bridge, they swim or wade across the Dhanei River every day in order to reach their school. I have a picture of them in my scrapbook. Holding books or satchels aloft in one hand, they do the breast stroke or dog-paddle with the other; or form a chain and help each other across.

Wherever you go in India, you will find children helping out with the family's source of livelihood, whether it be drying fish on the Malabar coast, or gathering saffron buds in Kashmir, or grazing camels or cattle in a village in Rajasthan or Gujarat.

Only the more fortunate can afford to send their children to English-medium private or 'public' schools, and those children really are fortunate, for some of these institutions are excellent schools, as good, and often better, than their counterparts in Britain or the US. Whether it's in Ajmer or Bangalore, New Delhi or Chandigarh, Kanpur or Calcutta, the best schools set very high standards. The growth of a prosperous middle class has led to an ever-increasing demand for quality education. But as private schools proliferate, standards suffer too, and many parents must settle for the second-rate.

The great majority of our children still attend schools run by the state or municipality. These vary from the good to the bad to the ugly, depending on how they are run and where they are situated. A classroom without windows, or with a roof that lets in the monsoon rain, is not uncommon. Even so, children from different communities learn to live and grow together. Hardship makes brothers of us all.

The census tells us that two in every five of the population is in the age group of five to fifteen. Almost half our population is on the way to school!

And here I stand at my window, watching some of them pass by—boys and girls, big and small, some scruffy, some smart, some mischievous, some serious, but all *going* somewhere—hopefully towards a better future.

READING WAS MY RELIGION

The RAF had undertaken to pay for my schooling, so I was able to continue at the Bishop Cotton School. Back in Shimla I found a sympathetic soul in Mr Jones, an ex-army Welshman who taught us divinity. He did not have the qualifications to teach us anything else, but I think I learnt more from him than from most of our more qualified staff. He had even got me to read the Bible (King James version) for the classical simplicity of its style.

Mr Jones got on well with small boys, one reason being that he never punished them. Alone among the philistines, he was the only teacher to stand out against corporal punishment. He waged a lone campaign against the custom of caning boys for their misdemeanours, and in this respect was thought to be little eccentric, and he lost his seniority because of his refusal to administer physical punishment.

But there was nothing eccentric about Mr Jones, unless it was the pet pigeon that followed him everywhere and sometimes perched on his bald head. He managed to keep the pigeon (and his cigar) out of the classroom, but his crowded, untidy bachelor quarters reeked of cigar smoke.

He had a passion for the works of Dickens, and when he discovered that I had *read Nicholas Nickleby* and *Sketches by Box,* he allowed me to look at his set of the *Complete Works,* with the illustrations by PMz. I launched into *David Copperfield,* which I thoroughly enjoyed, identifying myself with young David, his triumphs and tribulations. After reading *Copperfield* I decided it was a fine thing to be a writer. The seed had already been sown, and although in my imagination I still saw myself as an Arsenal goalkeeper or a Gene Kelly-type tap dancer, I think I knew in my heart that I was best suited to the written word. I was topping the class in essay writing; although I had an aversion to studying the texts that were prescribed for English Literature classes.

Mr Jones, with his socialist, Dickensian viewpoint, had an aversion to P.G. Wodehouse, whose comic novels I greatly enjoyed. He told me that these novels glamorized the most decadent aspects of upper-class; English life (which was probably true), and that only recently, during the war (when he was interned in France), Wodehouse had been making propaganda broadcasts on behalf of Germany. This was true, too; although years later when I read the texts of those broadcasts (in *Performing Fled),* they seemed harmless enough.

But Mr Jones did have a point. Wodehouse was hopelessly out of date, for when I went to England after leaving school, I couldn't find anyone remotely resembling a Wodehouse character—except perhaps Ukridge, who was always borrowing money from his friends in order to set up some business or the other. He was universal.

The school library, the Anderson Library, was fairly well-stocked, and it was to be something of a haven for me over the next three years. There were always writers, past or present, to 'discover'—and I still have a tendency to ferret out writers who have been ignored, neglected or forgotten.

After *Copperfield,* the novel that most influenced me was Hugh Walpole's *Fortitude,* an epic account of another young writer in the making. Its opening line still acts as a clarion call when I feel depressed or as though I am getting nowhere: 'Tisn't life that matters! Tis the courage you bring to it.'

Walpole's more ambitiousus works have been forgotten, but his stories and novels of the macabre are still worth reading—'Mr Perrin and Mr Traill', 'Portrait of a Man with Red Hair', 'The White Tower' and, of course, *Fortitude.* I returned to it last year and found it was still stirring stuff.

But life wasn't all books. At the age of fifteen I was at my best as a football goalkeeper, hockey player and athlete. I was also acting in school plays and taking part in debates. I wasn't much of a boxer—the sport I disliked—but I had learnt to use my head to good effect, and managed to get myself disqualified by butting the other fellow in the head or midriff. As all games were compulsory, I had to overcome my fear of water and learn to swim a little. Mr Jones taught me to do the breast stroke, saying it was more suited to my temperament than the splash and dash stuff.

The only thing I wouldn't do was sing, and although I loved listening to great singers, from Caruso to Gigli, I couldn't sing a note. Our music teacher, Mrs Knight, put me in the school choir because, she said, I looked like a choir boy, all pink and shining in a cassock and surplice, but she forbade me from actually singing. I was to open my mouth with the others, but on no account was I to allow any sound to issue from it.

This took me back to the convent in Mussoorie where I had been given piano lessons, probably at my father's behest. The nun who was teaching me would get so exasperated with my stubborn inability to strike the right chord or play the right notes that she would crack me over the knuckles with a ruler, thus effectively putting to an end any interest I might have had in learning to play a musical instrument. Mr Priestley's violin in prep-school, and now Mrs Knight's organ-playing were none too inspiring.

Insensitive though I may have been to high notes and low notes, *diminuendos* and *crescendos,* I was nevertheless sensitive to sound, such as birdsong, the hum of the breeze playing in tall trees, the rustle of autumn leaves, crickets chirping, water splashing and murmuring brooks, the sea sighing on the sand—all natural sounds, that indicated a certain harmony in the natural world.

Man-made sounds—the roar planes, the blare of horns, the thunder of trucks and engines, the baying of a crowd—are usually ugly, but some gifted humans have risen to create great music. We must not then scorn the also-rans, who come down hard on their organ pedals or emulate cicadas with their violin playing.

Although I was quite popular at BCS, after Omar's departure I did not have many close friends. There was, of course, young A, my junior by two years, who followed me everywhere until I gave in and took him to the pictures in town, or fed him at the tuck shop.

There were just one or two boys who actually read books for pleasure. We tend to think of that era as one when there were no distractions such as television, computer games and the like. But reading has always been a minority pastime. People say children don't read any more. This may be true of the vast majority, but I know many boys and girls who enjoy reading—far more than I encountered when I was a schoolboy. In those days there were comics and the radio and the cinema. I went to the cinema whenever I could, but that did not keep me from reading almost everything that came my way. And so it is today. Book readers are special people, and they will always turn to books as the ultimate pleasure. Those who do not read are the unfortunate ones. There's nothing wrong with them, but they are missing out on one of life's compensations and rewards. A great book is a friend that never lets you down. You can return to it again and again, and the joy first derived from it will still be there.

I think it is fair to say that, when I was a boy, reading was my true religion. It helped me discover my soul.